★ ★ ★

Mr. President, Why Don't You Paint Your White House Another Color!

★ ★ ★

Also by David Heller
★ ★ ★

DEAR GOD: WHAT RELIGION WERE THE DINOSAURS?

DEAR GOD: CHILDREN'S LETTERS TO GOD

TALKING TO YOUR CHILD ABOUT GOD

THE CHILDREN'S GOD

THE SOUL OF A MAN

"GROWING UP ISN'T HARD TO DO
IF YOU START OUT AS A KID"

Matthew (age 6)

Mr. President, Why Don't You Paint Your White House Another Color!

David Heller

Ballantine Books
New York

LIBRARY OF CONGRESS CATALOGING-IN-PUBLICATION DATA

Heller, David
Mr. President, why don't you paint your white house another
color! / [compiled by] David Heller. — 1st ed.
p. cm.
ISBN 0-345-36551-8
1. United States—Politics and government—Public opinion.
2. Public opinion—United States. 3. Children—United
States—Attitudes I. Title
JK261.H45   1991
320.973—dc20   90-93567
CIP

Text design by Beth Tondreau Design/Mary A. Wirth

Manufactured in the United States of America
First Edition: November 1991
10 9 8 7 6 5 4 3 2

★ ★ ★

TO MARCI AND MARISSA MELZER,
*My Expert Consultants on Young People
and Their Views of the World.*

AND TO THEIR MOTHER, SALLY,
*Who Made Certain
That They Were Available,
Even As I Deluged Them with Questions.*

Contents

★ ★ ★

Ronald Reagan

Darnell (age 12)

Preface
★ ★ ★

Dear President Bush,

Who is a stronger President? You or
President Reagan?

You should have an arm wrestle and see!

Bye,

Lou C. (age 11)

*T*hat clever letter was
authored by Lou as part of my interview with
him about America and the Presidency. Like
many of his fellow Americans—typical
youngsters between the ages of six and thirteen—Lou had developed some very ani-
mated views about our Presidents. Along
with the many other children whom I have
interviewed—girls and boys, black and white
children, Democrats and Republicans—Lou

was outspoken about our uniquely American form of government. These youngsters will tell you just how they see the world—the good, the bad, and even the totally uncool! So, Mr. Washington and Mr. Lincoln, and you, too, Mr. Bush and Mr. Quayle, take cover from the quick tongues of this younger generation.

Do kids really develop their own political and patriotic ideas? They most certainly do so. Through interviews, I have discovered that they speak about Presidents and politics with surprising familiarity, though their novel interpretations of presidential life are anything but routine and predictable. Unburdened by the sometimes parochial concerns of adults, and even the occasional apathy of adolescence, these pundits have a special knack for selecting out the salient issues of American life. We can learn bountifully from their visions of America and its Presidency, even if we must forgive them for confusing Gerald Ford with a car manufacturer or Lyndon Johnson with a restaurant chain owner!

★ ★ ★
The Children

The youngsters whose ideas and vision of America shape this book range in age from six to thirteen. They were contacted through public school teachers, their parents, and other individuals who work daily with children. While many were interviewed in classrooms, some were interviewed at their homes or in other suitable locations (e.g., a neighbor's home). Whenever feasible, the youngsters responded orally to those questions that required it.

The children reflect a considerable diversity, coming from all major racial groups and a variety of ethnic backgrounds. They lived in a number of geographic regions. Some lived in big cities; others in small towns. Some of their parents were Republicans, while other parents were longtime Democrats, and still others were Independents. Approximately the same number of boys was interviewed as girls.

All participants were asked to take part in a series of fun and imaginative tasks. These included: telling a story about a President, defining political and patriotic terms, offering opinions about famous figures and key issues, commenting about the everyday life of the President and his family, writing letters to the President, and often drawing a picture of a President.

No one loves to draw more than small children. Even the most reticent youngster loses his or her shyness if supplied with crayons or colored pencils. Youngsters' drawings tell us so much—not only about the Presidents but about children, too. What political attitudes are our youngsters developing? How do they picture the office of the Presidency? What characteristics of a President do they choose to emphasize? What I've done in this book is to take the youngsters' comments, opinions, and drawings, and edit them, including on the following pages those that were the most entertaining and thought-provoking, and which seemed to reflect the considerable variety of children's viewpoints.

Many times the children referred to the President as a "he"; I have done that occasionally as well. Please be assured that in no way do I mean to indicate that the Presidency should be held by men only. The use of "he" is intended only as a generic term consistent with our history thus far.

★ ★ ★

The Presidency from a Child's Viewpoint

Like those of many children of the 1960s, my own earliest memories include some very striking images of our nation's leaders. Some of my images of the Presidency were hopeful and idealistic; others were poignant and irrevocably painful. As with American children of any era, the Presidents meant a great deal to me. I identified with their triumphs and disappointments, and I cried a child's anguished tears at the loss of President Kennedy.

I was not yet three when John Kennedy's motorcade caravanned through my Connecticut hometown on a summer day in 1960, as part of his campaign route. I remember red, white, and blue banners and buttons that seemed to stretch on for as far as I could see. I can still recall the sense of excitement and anticipation. It was fun to catch a glimpse of the future President, and it was great to feel a part of this American parade.

Several years later I was in a first-grade classroom that was rifled with fear and confusion. Our teacher was uncontrollably mournful and school was about to be dismissed early. "What's going on?" my classmates and I wondered. For this one moment, the weekend was descending too soon. It was Friday, November 22, 1963. The country, and that entire room full of previously buoyant six-year-olds, would never be exactly the same again. Gone forever was the illusion of the invincible leader. It was as if everyone's father had been killed at once. As we struggled to understand this death over the next few days, we all felt part of a country in mourning—and it affected my view of the Presidency forever.

By the time I was ten, Vietnam and its coverage was a regular though unwelcome part of my television viewing. It was difficult for anyone, child or adult, to avoid the war and its impact—for television brought it home in a frightening and overwhelming way, especially for the children. I remember President Johnson's speeches to the nation and his inevitable rise and fall. I recall wondering what President Nixon would be like. I wasn't at all certain that I still wanted to be President someday, and I felt a young boy's concern for his country. Where was America headed?

That concern has never wavered. I am still taken

with the question of our nation's direction: What does the future hold as we head toward the twenty-first century? These vivid childhood memories I described to you still intrigue me, for I can sense their enduring impact on my life. They remind me that children are profoundly influenced by our government and our Presidents. My own memories stir a similar curiosity about today's young people. How do they feel about America? How do they picture our nation's leaders and make sense of these changing and confusing times?

These are some of the fundamental concerns that moved me to compile *Mr. President.* I have chosen to concentrate on the more lighthearted aspects of children's ideas for a specific purpose. Like the rest of us, children express their truest thoughts and feelings while "letting go"—as they spontaneously joke or philosophize about life. Through this emphasis on humor, I do not in any way mean to suggest that the youngsters' ideas are silly or trivial. On the contrary, children have a political understanding in their own right and should be invited to speak their minds far more often and in whatever manner they choose. They have so much to teach us about politics, patriotism, and the Presidents we select to lead us.

Please join me in enjoying and learning from what these children have to say. Through the living drama and color of their original ideas, we can discover a great deal about the kinds of leaders and the kind of world we are providing for them. How often the ideas of young people seem to reflect the trends and moods and heartbeat of our nation. The kids will make you laugh, but they'll make you think, too. I guess that's one reason I love them.

David Heller, Ph.D.
Boston

Abraham Lincoln

J.P.
(age 9)

Introduction
★ ★ ★

"We, the Little People . . ."

*About the Children
and What They Are Saying*

Kids certainly say the darndest political things—not only about the Presidency but also about American life. Their comments, letters, and drawings stay with you, as you find yourself bemused and entertained by them. As someone who has been privy to their thoughts, I've formed some general impressions of how youngsters think politically and what they are trying to say. It is my pleasure to share some of these observations with you.

What follow are not the research findings of a statistician but the real-world impressions of a writer. While these observations may lack technical definitiveness, they express an appreciation of children as individuals—as little adults with their own special thoughts and feelings. While I've selected the most humorous and poignant children's comments, I've tried to learn from all of my interviewees and their thoughtful ideas. In the budding political viewpoints of these youngsters, I have found much wisdom and food for thought along with the humor. The children are complex. They are at once innocent and yet sophisticated, liberal in some ways and yet conservative in others, and patriotic and rebellious all at the same time. Their paradoxical nature makes them all the more fascinating, and quite a study for the adult interviewer or reader.

★ ★ ★

Where Do Those Lively Ideas Come From?

Children's political ideas represent a blend of early learning, opinion, and a generous portion of make-believe. Despite the factual oversights in some of their accounts, much of what they say rings of political truth. In their driving curiosity we can observe a sincere pursuit of truth. Children want to know what's happening in the big adult world beyond their immediate homes and neighborhoods. It's this curiosity that motivates them to seek out new political information and hearsay, and come up with some coherent version of how the world works.

"I learned most of this stuff about the Presidents on my own," says ten-year-old Sean in a manner that brings a young Lincoln to mind. "But I guess I learned a few things in social studies at school."

I believe that Sean is correct to suggest that youngsters can learn a lot on their own, although his allusion to other influences is equally important. Schools, parents, television, and the media all seem to play significant roles in the development of children's political ideas.

Schools are responsible for providing a historical context for current political affairs, and they teach kids about the American philosophy of government. Children seem to assimilate these basic facts and beliefs, and, more often than not, take them as their own. The relationship between long-standing American institutions, such as the Constitution, and current American politics and trends is not always clear to the children, but they do their best to perceive a connection. National holidays like President's Day, Veteran's Day, and Martin Luther King Day inspire additional learning in the schools, as youngsters often become excited by the color and pageantry of the holidays. It's too bad that Independence Day occurs on the Fourth of July, when school is not in session, for the youngsters are not as available for the patriotic and political lessons that could be taught . . . although I must admit that most of my interviewees would cringe at the thought of school in July!

Parents might well have the most penetrating influence on the children's political preferences. If you find a staunch Republican or a steadfast Democrat under the age of thirteen, chances are that a strong parental influence is at work. Around election time or at other times, a mother or father may voice a strong political sentiment about the President, about taxes, or about the local political parties. Children hear their attitudes and begin to mimic their parents, particularly if the views are expressed with considerable passion or vehemence. Hence, during interviews, youngsters would occasionally use borrowed phrases like: "He wouldn't be good for the country" or "He would raise our taxes." Interestingly, many of the most outspoken youngsters, children who defined themselves as strongly for one party or the other, had one parent who stood out as a political role model. That parent's influence was considerable, as the child was inspired by the forcefulness of his or her parent's views.

Along with other socializing factors, television and the mass media are hardly minor background influences. On the contrary, television frequently seemed to be the primary source of political information for kids. How often the youngsters would say: "I saw the President on television and he looked . . ." While some children may be affected by what television commentators have to say, I doubt that news analysis had the highest degree of salience for most of the kids. Rather, it's the *images* of the President and other key figures that catch their attention, as well as how those leaders act on television. These graphic pictures are easier to appreciate and understand, and are more colorful for the children as well. Youngsters are enthralled with these images much as they are with television figures, but there's a difference: Even the most naive children realize that the President is real and not a fictitious character— and that moves the youngsters to fantasize about a President's life long after the television set is shut off.

Schools, parents, and television—all are central factors in the creation and development of children's political ideas. But that's not where the process of political learning ends. For children are more than blank slates or mere recipients of other people's ideas and images. Youngsters do collect all the information they can from other people, but then they begin to churn it over in their own minds. They sort out what they like from what they don't like; they distinguish what's important to them from what might be incidental. And since they sometimes take in only bits and pieces of relevant information, children are inclined to embellish and to take educated guesses about political affairs.

Moreover, a child's personality is too powerful a force not to influence newly discovered political ideas. Information about the President and other leaders is shaped and colored depending upon a youngster's current personality needs and interests. Some youngsters may be predisposed to focus on the fatherly functions of a President because they are curious about a father's role. Others might concentrate on the humanitarian chores of the President because they are socially inclined. Still others may focus on the high-profile position of the President because they admire the attention that accompanies the office. In this way, the development of a child's political view is a highly individualized process, far more involved and complicated than a parrotlike adoption of established views alone.

Each youngster weaves his or her own political tapestry; the interviewing process I used was one means of seeing how the intricate weaving takes shape. It was a helpful way to enter into the child's inner world. The children's responses are a testament to their originality and inventiveness, as well as a sign of the political knowledge they are beginning to acquire.

★ ★ ★

Children's Images of the President

Through their witty and amusing answers, children also reveal how they view the Presidency. If you look at their responses closely, you can begin to piece together what the children picture as they speak about the President.

Depending upon their own personalities, and, of course, who is currently in office, young people describe a number of common images. How do most children picture the President? Some imagine a "Grand Commander," a powerful figure whose role is to issue mandates for everyone else in the country to follow. Such youngsters emphasize the status of the President and the considerable privileges of his office, depicting the President as a lone decision maker who always has the final word. For instance, seven-year-old Carol states: "The President is in charge of everything, even where all the treasury is stored. He gives other people orders and they go out to collect the taxes and run the schools." Meanwhile, ten-year-old Charles notes: "President Bush has a big limo and gives all the instructions from his limo phone!"

Other young people envision the President as a "Great Protector." These children see the President as a strong and benevolent leader who looks out for the interests of the United States and good people everywhere. In their view, the President's primary role is to defend the nation against threats to freedom or challenges to our well-being. "He keeps the peace and makes sure that criminals get locked up," explains Jenny, age seven. Nine-year-old Keith surmises: "The President is supposed to keep drugs out of the country and make sure they stay in South America."

A third popular image of the President is as a "Super Politician." Some youngsters imagine a boss figure who runs the country with an iron hand and whose primary concern is political advantage. This President is preoccupied with his control over the electorate and with his own reelection. A cigar-wielding type, the President is often seen campaigning and talking "a-mile-a-minute." He's usually pictured as slick and clever but rarely as substantive and sincere. Camille, age nine, provides an example: "The Presidents are always taking polls to find out what the people want to hear. Then they have their speech writers write them a speech that pleases the people—so that they can stay as President. . . . I don't think they can stay there forever, though."

Yet another presidential image may be either a result of media socialization or a manifestation of the modern Presidency itself. Some children picture a national leader who acts like "Mr. President, the TV Star." These young people describe an amicable and social President who enjoys a bit of drama and an attentive national audience. The whole world is a stage to this flashy Chief Executive who seeks fame and accolades as much as power. It's a presidential figure whose main goal is to be the most famous person of his era, a lofty status derived from his high-profile position. Ted, age nine, comments: "I thought President Reagan was nice, but he acted too much. . . . But maybe all the Presidents like to be on television," while the curious Mindy, age seven, offers: "I wonder if the President practices a lot before he gives a big speech. I would get nervous if I was the President. I don't like to be on the stage."

While these are some of the general presidential images that children suggest by their responses, the ideas of young people can be further affected by their age. When I consider their responses by age, I find that it provides a window into how concepts of the

Presidency develop over time. Age differences are not hard-and-fast indicators that pertain to every individual child, but they do provide us with a rough picture of how many children think about the White House and its most prominent residents.

Younger children (ages six to eight) tend to see the President in unqualified and usually positive terms. They often speak about the President with great respect and see the President as more than a regular person in an important position. Sometimes it seems that the President is more of a national icon to them. For example, six-year-old Barbara told me in her interview: "We should all do what the President asks us to, because he is like General George Washington, the father of our country."

These youngsters may not see any limit or scope to the President's power. They may perceive his authority as boundless. On many occasions, these children acknowledged that they think about how exciting a President's life is. "A President must have it *real* good," says eight-year-old Corey, "especially since he doesn't have to do things like take out the garbage." Corey and his cohorts are not at all focused on the possible headaches and liabilities of the job, preferring instead to concentrate on its fringe benefits.

Children between the ages of nine and eleven differ somewhat from their younger and more innocent brothers and sisters. "I worry that everybody is going to die from drugs," acknowledges nine-year-old Will. "I would like to ask President Bush what he is doing about the homeless and the environment," explains Elizabeth T., age ten.

Nine- and ten-year-olds like Will and Elizabeth are frequently very inquisitive. They see problems like drug abuse and the plight of the homeless and they want to know what is being done about it. While they are unlikely to confront the President in an overtly critical manner, they are not reticent about bringing up controversial issues. These middle youngsters are clearly in a learning mode, receptive to whatever they can ascertain about the real world of government. In their developing maturity they are beginning to consider the adult world more carefully, and the Presidency and all that it touches is an important part of that world.

My oldest interviewees, those young people between eleven and thirteen years of age, were the most likely to imagine the President in skeptical, or in some cases, negative, terms. They were also the most opinionated. Not only did they freely address issues of war and peace or pressing social problems, but they also demonstrated great sophistication about political motives and actions. In general, they saw the President as a human figure who was not perfect. They seemed to realize that a President is required to balance a variety of interests, including his own political power. Thirteen-year-old James comments: "A President has got to do a lot of wheeling and dealing if he wants to stay on top. I don't mean he has to be a crook, but he's got to pick the right people and be careful what he says."

More than a few older children see American government and the Presidency in philosophical terms. "I wonder if a President ever gets lonely," observes twelve-year-old Carlos. "I think President Bush must feel like he has the whole world on his shoulders sometimes," surmises eleven-year-old Krista. Such comments come from young people preparing to take their government a bit more seriously, and perhaps readying themselves to understand the Presidency in all its aspects. No longer do these older youngsters see the Presidency in simple or one-dimensional terms. They are beginning to appreciate the confluence of events and personalities that shape the course of American leadership, and how difficult a job the Presidency really is.

"President Bush Should Hire a Secretary of Peace!"

Children's Political Commentary

*W*hether children are learning their politics and government from their parents, schools, or television, they are certainly acquiring some passionate ideas about America and about the world. When you ask kids to venture a political opinion, they might say just about anything! But there's one thing that you can count on: Children will defend their opinions about our leaders and most pressing issues with vehemence and resolve.

Consider what would happen if we asked youngsters their views on famous political figures like President Bush or Vice President Quayle. Or foreign leaders like Mikhail Gorbachev or former British Prime Minister Margaret Thatcher. And what about other prominent and well-known people, like the Reagans or Rev. Jesse Jackson?

Children are equally opinionated about controversial situations and issues. They like to talk about current events, whether the events are taking place nearby or in the far reaches of the globe. While some of their ideas may be humorous, their assessment of serious problems is often thought-provoking. They speak about the Middle East or South Africa with great curiosity and concern; in some cases they convey outrage or upset. The same is true for their feelings about our own cities and towns, where issues of the homeless and drug abuse have these empathic youngsters concerned.

The alacrity with which kids offer their honest opinions is sometimes startling. Their eagerness to respond to commentary questions, as well as the content of their responses themselves, suggest that children are far more than miniature facsimiles of their parents. As youngsters watch the presidential campaigns, the President's speeches, and the unfolding of international events, they pick up things from adults, but they also think for themselves. They are *active interpreters* of American and international dramas. Children place their own spin on the people and events that shape our lives, and now we can all be privy to what they have to say.

★ ★ ★
Famous Political People

What Is Your Opinion of Them?

1. About President George Bush

"He is a colorful guy for sure. I like the way he dresses and the hilarious jokes he tells."

(BO, AGE 9)

"George Bush is a geek. He tries too hard to be a regular guy. But he's still kind of an egghead."

(LORETTA, AGE 12)

"He is a kind and gentle man who wants what's best for the country and is working hard to make things better for the kids of America." (JOHN, AGE 9)

"He is a sneak just like George Washington and Boy George!" (CAL, AGE 11)

"How come I never saw him in a war helmet or a war uniform?" (ROSS, AGE 8)

"He is a good leader to have around in case some crazy guy attacks you." (VANCE, AGE 9)

"It must have been hard for him to be in a war and have a wife with a broken leg at the same time . . . She shouldn't go sledding any more."

(CHANDRA, AGE 9)

"I'm waiting to see what he does in the next seven years. Then I'll make my decision."

(MARINA, AGE 12)

"My view is that he is too easy on criminals. I am for tough penalties. If they deal with drugs, they should get less food. . . . He should speak about it more."

(STACEY, AGE 12)

"He is a good President and he deserves all of our supports. We should send him money if he needs it."

(LINDA, AGE 8)

"President Bush is a very good President. He stood up to the Iraqi man who was against the whole world and even the United Nations."

(JASON G., AGE 10)

"I blame him for getting us into a war. We have no business being in Saudi Arabia. We should buy our oil from some place like Bermuda."

(KAYE, AGE 8)

"At first, I didn't know what he meant about making a line in the sand . . . but now I know."

(AFTON, AGE 12)

"In my opinion, George Bush is a decent man but not a true leader. I hope that he can show more leadership by stating his values. And by getting out there himself and cleaning the environment. He should pick up a shovel!" (CARLO, AGE 13)

"I think he is too corny. He always seems to be clowning around. We need a person who is serious."
(BARBARA, AGE 11)

"George Bush is okay for a boy."
(CASSANDRA, AGE 8)

"You always see him on those fishing trips on the weekends. . . . I wonder if he ever catches anything."
(RANDY, AGE 11)

"He's nice. He's doing his best. But if he turns out to be bad at the job, we should find something else for him to do. Maybe he could have a department store."
(JENNIFER F., AGE 9)

"I think he tries real hard and he wants peace. He wishes things were different, but he knows that sometimes you have to stick up for people who can't pay for their own army." (BETTY, AGE 8)

"I know he feels bad that some of our soldiers died . . . He should let it out and cry."
(TESS, AGE 8)

"I wonder if he is biting his nails because we have so much of the army so far away."
(DANIEL M., AGE 8)

"He is a very friendly dude, but how come he doesn't say what he means instead of asking people to read his lips? . . . I don't blame him for hating those green vegetables, though." (REGINALD, AGE 10)

2. About Barbara Bush

"She's all right, but she makes me think of my second grade teacher, Mrs. Malley, and Mrs. Malley gave me a POOR in math!" (KENDRA, AGE 10)

"I think she looks like one of those ladies on 'The Golden Girls' TV show." [WHICH ONE?] "The one with the white hair." (SANDY, AGE 9)

"Barbara must read real good, because she's always nagging kids to read better." (SHEILA, AGE 8)

"She is the worst of all the people in Washington because she is smart enough to know better than be a phony. . . . She tries to act like she is just one of us, but she really is rich like anything."

(CORINNE, AGE 8)

"Barbara is cool. I don't mind her. She doesn't act rich or stuck up." (TAWNY, AGE 12)

"I feel that Barbara Bush will be a much better First Lady than Nancy Reagan was. Nancy Reagan was too conceited. Also, Barbara Bush has grandchildren my age. She probably cares about kids."

(ALEX, AGE 10)

"She might be better than George Bush. I think it is time for a girl to be President. I wish one of these wives would run and beat the husbands in a landslide!" (TONI, AGE 8)

"She is the President's wife and she sews the flags at the White House. . . . At least until she gets tired."
(BEVERLY, AGE 6)

"I don't have much to say about her. Just that she has pearly white teeth!" (MARCI, AGE 13)

3. About Vice President Dan Quayle

"People should give him a chance to make his mistakes before they call him names. You have to wait till he screws up." (FRANK, AGE 9)

"He is a little nice but not too much."
(CORINNE, AGE 8)

"My mother said he chases after girls."
(VINCENT, AGE 9)

"He wants to be President someday, but I don't think he's a big, tough guy at all. . . . He looks like a sissy to me!" (WALTER, AGE 10)

"I thought his name was Mike Quayle. Maybe I was wrong. I haven't seen that much of him, so it is hard to say what he is like. Where is he?"
(KYLE, AGE 11)

"Dan Quayle is young, and that is good. But he's kind of a dork, and that is not." (LISA, AGE 10)

"He reminds me of my friend Jason's father. He is kind of snappy and smart, but sometimes I don't understand what he is saying." (MIKE, AGE 10)

"I think he is kind of cute and would make a good husband to somebody. . . . Like my sister Janice." [HOW OLD IS JANICE?] "She just turned fourteen."

(ELIZA, AGE 9)

"All the kids at school make fun of Quayle. They say he's just a bird and stuff like that."

(KENNY L., AGE 7)

"I like him because he is from Indiana and that's where they have good basketball, with Coach Bob Knight. Is everyone from there like that?"

(ANDREW, AGE 11)

"I wonder how Quayle will do if he is in charge of drugs. I hope he is very experienced about drugs because we have to just say no." (MARY, AGE 9)

4. About Marilyn Quayle

"Who is she, an actress?" (DAWN M., AGE 8)

"She is married to Dan Quayle and must be happy because he is the Vice President. . . . She has been pretty quiet so far, but just wait, she will want to talk!" (VINCENT, AGE 9)

"I hear that she is a good mom. I also heard she likes kids a lot. Like Mrs. Bush. Then she is okay as far as I can see." (MAUREEN, AGE 8)

"I think she is pretty. Her posters with her blond hair and her dress flying up are all over the place."

(BART, AGE 11)

"Dan Quayle must love her a lot for putting up with him. He's such a jerk!" (ROBIN, AGE 11)

"She looks like she is right out of the 1950s, like she might be on 'Leave It To Beaver' or something."
(SUE ELLEN, AGE 11)

"She doesn't seem to be involved with things. She should be. Otherwise when she is first lady she won't know what to do. She should get some help from Mrs. Bush or the Reagan lady." (TED, AGE 11)

5. About Ronald Reagan

"I am sorry that he is not the President anymore. He was good at acting like a President should."
(STAN, AGE 9)

"His head was flat!" (MARVIN, AGE 10)

"I think those cardboard cutouts of him they sell are real funny!" (CATHY, AGE 11)

"He was an excellent President. He should be on money." (TYLER, AGE 11)

"Who was he?" (JOJO, AGE 6)

"He was good for the country because he made Americans feel good about the country again . . . even if we don't feel so good about the rest of the violence in the world." (ABBY, AGE 12)

"He was President when I was born. . . . I like him!"
(JOEY, AGE 7)

"It seemed like he was President forever. Maybe not forever, but it seemed like a long, long time."
(RODERICK, AGE 13)

"Ronald Reagan is okay, but he joked too much. He should have been more serious and then maybe he would have got something done for the people."
(WILLIE, AGE 10)

"Reaganomics—I remember when you used to hear that word all the time. He invented it." [WHAT DO YOU THINK IT MEANS?] "I don't know. Maybe it's like recipes. It sounds like 'home economics.'"
(JERI, AGE 11)

6. About Nancy Reagan

"I admire her because she married someone who became the President." (KERI, AGE 13)

"She was Ronald Ragoon's wife." [RAGOON?] "Yeah, the guy who was the President before Bush took over." (JOHN, AGE 8)

"Didn't he have a wife before her?"
(JERI, AGE 11)

"Too many people are against her. I don't see why. . . . She seems like a nice old lady!" [WELL, I'M SURE SHE WOULD APPRECIATE YOUR SUP-

PORT.] "Well, I'm just being fair to her."
(NATE, AGE 10)

"She should get along better with her kids!"
(SUE ELLEN, AGE 11)

"She tries to get publicity in *The National Enquirer* too much!" (ROSEANNE, AGE 9)

"She is like a grandmother to all the people."
(JEN, AGE 7)

"I feel that she was nice. She had style and was elegant and kept the White House clean and pretty. Some of the wives are not ready for the job like she was." (CAMILLE, AGE 13)

"People say she is nosy, but I say what else is there to do if you are in the White House? Go bowling?"
(BYRON, AGE 10)

"I think she did a lot for women. She was a good speaker for women. I don't know all the details, but I think she was." (REGINA, AGE 11)

"She said no to drugs, so I am in favor of her."
(LEA, AGE 11)

"What did she do before she was a President's wife?"
(ALIYAH, AGE 9)

"I got no opinion worth mentioning on her."
(VINCENT, AGE 9)

"I heard that she had a book now. I want to read it because I want to know how you become a First Lady. Also, it might have gossip in it."

(GINA, AGE 12)

"I miss her." (MARY JO, AGE 10)

"I hope she is feeling good and is having a good time with Ron Reagan. I know they like to ride horses, so maybe she is getting off on that, now that they don't have to run the country anymore."

(SEAN, AGE 10)

"People named Nancy are always in first place."

(NANCY K., AGE 8)

7. About Mikhail Gorbachev

"He's that guy from Russia who is on TV a lot. . . . They sure show him a lot." (JOHN, AGE 8)

"He has a funny bald head. How did that Russian guy get that blotch on his head?" (TED, AGE 11)

"I don't trust him. I bet he drinks vodka and tells lies all the time." (NATALIE, AGE 13)

"I don't know who he is. Was he a Vice President?"

(JAN, AGE 8)

"I feel he is trying to make the world better, but I don't know if it will work. Some Communist might be out to get him." (GINA, AGE 11)

"Gorbyhead should have his own TV show!"
(ERIC K., AGE 10)

"He should visit here more times and see how much fun all of our cities are. . . . It beats Moscow any day."
(BRYN, AGE 9)

"I am not sure about him. Maybe he is good, but maybe he is not. The best way to tell is to see how he acts when he's with the President. See whether he's friendly or not. Then you can tell."
(ROLAND, AGE 11)

"Gorba-chop is a Russian leader who came to America last year and tried to play up to everybody. But we didn't fall for it." (GLYNNIS, AGE 11)

"He's a general on the other side."
(CHUCKIE, AGE 9)

"He's all right. He's a lot like President Bush, but he has less hair and can't speak a word of English."
(SUE, AGE 12)

8. About Raisa Gorbachev

"She is pretty Russian if you ask me."
(ROBIN, AGE 11)

"Her hats are nice and she dresses pretty well."
(AMY, AGE 11)

"I don't know why everybody makes a big deal of it because she wears a fur coat. She's just trying to fit in." (MOOKIE, AGE 11)

"I've heard of her, but I've never seen her. Does he keep her locked up or something?"

(ALEXIA, AGE 9)

"I wonder what her role is. Does she give her husband advice, like about weapons and nuclear war?"

(GERALD, AGE 9)

"Next time she visits the U.S., she should go to a movie or a concert. She would want to live here then, but she might miss all the fish they eat there. . . . She would have to live near the water so she could go out to fish restaurants that have the fish that costs a ton." (JESSIE, AGE 10)

"Does she have a spot on her head, too?"

(NAME WITHHELD FOR FEAR OF KGB RETALIATION; ALIAS TED, AGE 11)

9. Saddam Hussein

"We should have said to him: 'I don't like your moustache. If you don't get out of Kuwait, I'm going to pull your handlebars right off!'"

(MITCHELL, AGE 10)

"I would tell him: 'Give us more oil, you jerk! We're running out of gas!'" (KEVIN G., AGE 8)

"He should go jogging instead of invading other countries. Jogging would have helped him work off the tension." (JAN B., AGE 8)

"Didn't anybody ever teach him to respect other people's property. He is supposed to be the Iraq President, but he kidnapped people. What kind of parents did he have, anyway?" (ROBERTA T., AGE 10)

"I would have said to him: 'Let's make peace, Mr. Leader. Look, you can have some of these brownies my mother made . . . Don't worry, there's no bombs in them.'" (ANDREA P., AGE 8)

"That January 15th was a big date. He should have listened." (ELLEN, AGE 9)

"His mother wears combat boots . . . I bet she does, because he put his whole country into the army." (PETE R., AGE 9)

"He talked about milk factories a lot . . . What was his problem?" (SETH, AGE 10)

"I would have liked him better if he was one of the nice men who wears a towel around his head." (MARIE H., AGE 8)

"I kinda feel sorry for him because I don't think he is such a healthy person." (DON, AGE 8)

"I would have punched him out." (KEVIN B., AGE 12)

"They say he is a bad dictator who should be stopped. President Bush is against bad dictators." (AFTON, AGE 12)

"I bet they still hate him in Kuwait."
(GEORGE E., AGE 11)

"He reminds me of the Grinch."
(CHANDRA, AGE 9)

"I heard of him, but I can't remember where."
(LITA, AGE 7)

"That Iraq is a mean country. Maybe the people are not all mean, but they should never elect somebody like that Saddam again." (ANDREW, AGE 9)

"I didn't like Saddam Hussein when I saw him patting that little kid on the head. That kid didn't want to be there. He was no 'guest'. . . . The kid probably wanted to be playing soccer or something, not playing in jail." (JASON G., AGE 10)

"That Saddam person is a fat general who just likes to pick on smaller countries . . . He probably used to spit at the teachers when he was in school."
(RYAN, AGE 11)

10. King Faud and the Emir of Kuwait

"I think they are probably poker players."
(RUSSELL, AGE 10)

"King Fat? Is that his name? You got to be kidding."
(ROSS, AGE 8)

"The first one, the king, might be somebody in a fairy tale. The second one could be somebody who works in the king's palace." (ANNA, AGE 7)

"I think they are two of the Arab leaders and they sent us an invitation to come visit them . . . But then while we were there, everyone was surprised that a war started." (CHANDRA, AGE 9)

"I might have seen them in a movie . . . the one where the guy is always using his whip to knock people down . . . Indiana Jones."
(EUGENE K., AGE 9)

"They might be friends of Saddam Hussein, so they might be our enemies. I don't know for sure. There is probably an enemies list where you can check it out. But you got to know the telephone number so you can hear the list." (HALLEY, AGE 10)

"They own a lot of oil wells. But they aren't from Texas or anywhere near it. They are from other countries . . . I think Kuwait might be somewhere near Russia." (JAKE, AGE 10)

11. Rev. Jesse Jackson

"He is a great reverend and he should stick to it!"
(MARILYN, AGE 12)

"He talks good, and that's why people shut off the music on their radios when they go to one of his speeches." (WALTER, AGE 10)

"I love him because of all the good he does for all the people." (MELANIE, AGE 9)

"He's a well-known singer who also dances."
(VINCENT, AGE 9)

"I don't like him. I think he has a big ego. Plus he's getting old." (SEAN, AGE 10)

"He might get elected President someday. With all the times he's tried, he ought to win once!"
(DANNY, AGE 11)

"KEEP HOPE ALIVE! That's what he always says. But he needs some new ad men to get the message out." (TUCKER, AGE 12)

"He is a Democrat who hates the Republicans because they don't care about black people. . . . But he doesn't always get along with the Democrats either, so I hope he doesn't feel left out."
(PIA, AGE 13)

12. About Col. Oliver North

"You always see stuff about him in the *Daily News,* so he must be an entertainer or something important." (JOHN, AGE 8)

"He should be the next President!"
(VINCENT, AGE 9)

"North is the leader of the marines and a big hero because of it." (BART, AGE 11)

"He is a traitor because he ratted on the President—Reagan, not Bush. He is guilty. He should be in jail.

And he should stay there till he changes or else."
(ANNIE, AGE 11)

"I don't know much about him, but he says he is innocence, and who are we to say that he is a crook?"
(VIOLET H., AGE 13)

"I think it is a sad story . . . very sad for the whole U.S.A. . . . What exactly did he do?"
(MICHELLE, AGE 10)

"I know who he is. But he ain't no GI Joe. He just did what was good for himself and he didn't care about anybody else." (KELVIN, AGE 10)

"Ollie for President! My friend has one of those T-shirts. Could he run, or do you have to be in politics to run? What about Reagan? Was he in politics before? I don't think so."
(GEORGE R., AGE 11)

13. Former Prime Minister Margaret Thatcher

"I don't know about her. The only girl I can think of is the one in the *Tom Sawyer* book. Is that who you mean? I didn't know she grew up to be a prime minister. Was that in another book?"
(SHAUNA, AGE 10)

"She's a real prune-face. She's ugly! I don't like her."
(CLYDE, AGE 8)

"She has been there a long time, so I guess her people must like her. It is good for women to be ministers and Presidents, too, even if they are old like she is. It is never too late." (KELLY, AGE 12)

"I feel she is a nice lady. She is probably a friend of Diane, Charles's lady. They might play polo together." (ARN, AGE 10)

"I wish she would tell George Bush that we should have a woman as President here. She should say that we are too conservative here. We need a change."
(AMANDA, AGE 13)

"What country does she belong to? Are they friends with us or the enemy?" (CHARLENE, AGE 9)

"I wonder if she is descended down from the ones we fought to get our independence. No surprise that we didn't like them at all." (PETER G., AGE 13)

14. PLO Leader Yassir Arafat

"Who is he and why do people make fun of him by calling him 'fat'?" (WINNIE, AGE 10)

"He must be a foreigner. I don't think he was a senator or anything." (HARLEY, AGE 10)

"I know who he is. He is against Israel. So I don't trust him. What's his beef?" (DANIEL, AGE 12)

"He has a right to stand up for his people."
(SUE, AGE 12)

"He looks like somebody in that *Lawrence of Arabia* movie. One of the guys with the swords."

(BART, AGE 11)

"Why doesn't he ever shave?"

(KERI L., AGE 11)

"What is the PLO? Is it a religious group for people of the Protestant religion?" (SAM O., AGE 9)

"He might be the leader of another country. Is it China? No, probably not. Their names are different. Maybe he is Italian. He could be from there and live near the Pope." (LISA, AGE 10)

"I don't know who he is, but he might be part of a secret spy ring. . . . If he spies on President Bush, then I'm against him. Besides, I don't like people who keep secrets." (VINCENT, AGE 9)

"He's a terrorist. Send him to Alcatraz!"

(FRANK, AGE 9)

★ ★ ★

Political Topics and Issues
Where Do You Stand on Them?

1. The Nuclear Arms Race

"We should have a big foot race instead."

(VINCENT, AGE 9)

"Bombs are no way to talk to people."
(SARI, AGE 10)

"It's getting better. All the sides except the terrorists want to put down their weapons. We should have more cultural stuff between the sides, like boxing and rock music." (LEE, AGE 12)

"I'm glad that it might be all over. That kind of race is no good at all. . . . You don't get a trophy even if you win." (BARRY, AGE 12)

"You don't hear as much about nuclear arms now. All the talk is about peace. That's good. Like my father says, 'No news is good news!'"
(PETER J., AGE 13)

"Nuclear *anything* is bad. . . . Look at that Seasbrook place. I wouldn't want to live near any nuclear stuff." (CARIN, AGE 9)

"I feel America should be ready for any kind of war. We need strong defenses so everyone can be at peace." (SPIKE, AGE 11)

"Too many countries have nuclear weapons now. What if a crazy country like Iran or China started something? I don't know what we should do, but if we could steal their bombs, we should go ahead and do that. That kind of stealing is okay."
(CARTER, AGE 12)

"I hope we can stop the killing so we can get on with working and making money and resting."
(MARINA, AGE 12)

"I don't think there's any place that's dumb enough to explode a nuclear bomb. It would be crazy. . . . Well, maybe there are some crazy places down in the South somewhere." [IN THE SOUTH?] "You know, like around New Orleans." (GAYLE, AGE 10)

"The Bomb was really a big bomb. . . . Next time the scientists should find something useful!"
(CHARLIE F., AGE 12)

2. The War in the Persian Gulf

"Let's play news . . . This is a newscast . . . 'Israel was bombed today.' . . . Now back to you, Tom . . . Film later at eleven." (CAREY H., AGE 6)

"The TV people shouldn't tell too much. The other people could hear it and learn our secrets . . . They shouldn't be tattletales." (BETTY, AGE 8)

"I am scared by the Gulf War. They shouldn't scare kids like that. With wars. Some of the people running their countries aren't too nice."
(SUSIE T., AGE 7)

"Nobody should have sent those scuds and those exorcedrin missiles to Iraq . . . That was stupid!"
(TIM P., AGE 13)

"There is too much death in the world. It was good that we had a prayer day. God must do something about these wars and we could help him."
(RYAN, AGE 11)

"Why do they call it the 'Persian War'? Are there a lot of cats there?" (MELODY, AGE 8)

"I don't like it. I don't understand too much about it. I know that the Iraqs were wrong to beat up the other country so bad. But that's all I know. The rest of the stuff gives me a big headache and it makes me want to cry . . . people are killing each other."
(TAMMY G., AGE 10)

"I know that the Congress voted for it, but did they really check with the people first? Nobody called my parents. They would have said: 'No, stay here in the U.S.A. Don't go fight Iraq!'"
(CLAIRE, AGE 11)

"I don't like war. It scares me. I don't know why it doesn't scare older people." (DANIEL M., AGE 8)

"We are the winners. No doubt about it. We have better men." (GEORGE E., AGE 11)

"My cousin is in the sand . . . I am afraid Mr. Hussein will hurt him." (LIZ D., AGE 8)

"We go the right to be there. They were hogs with our oil." (TESS, AGE 8)

"I hated to see those people with gas masks. It looked like a scary science movie." (CHANDRA, AGE 9)

"The reporters with the gas masks on looked strange, and it was hard to hear them talk . . . You can bet they must be getting good salaries to do that." (PEDRO, AGE 12)

"I would like to be a pilot one of these days, but I wouldn't like to get shot down and be a prisoner."
(JASON G., AGE 10)

"Saddam Hussein should be arrested by the American police." (BARBARA Y., AGE 9)

"Where do we keep all those bombs here in the United States? It must be in the mountains in a secret hiding place, because you never see them around here." (DANIEL M., AGE 8)

"The Gulf War is not funny and it makes you feel like that there are some nut cases in the world . . . They should have a Golf War and the people could fight with the golf clubs or maybe they could play the others for about eighteen holes."
(LEN O., AGE 13)

3. The Middle East (in general)

"There's more trouble there than there is in our schoolyard at recess." (NORM, AGE 7)

"I wish the Israels and the Arabics could get along better . . . I hope Israel don't take those scuddy bombs too personal." (JASON G., AGE 10)

"They have too many weapons in the middle east. They should shoot some of them all the way to the moon!" (DANIEL M., AGE 8)

"It's a war over there. I'm sure glad I don't live in Afranistan." (CLINT, AGE 9)

"We should leave them all alone and let them be mean to each other if they want. They will get tired of it. Just like my brother and me."
(CRAIG, AGE 10)

"Mideast? Do you mean like Ohio and Illinois?"
(JAN, AGE 9)

"Israel is our only friend there. It is important for the U.S. that Israel survives. We should send them more food and as many anti-Arab tanks as they need." (BARRY, AGE 12)

"We should hold all of them hostage like they do to Americans!" (JERI, AGE 11)

"I would separate all the countries more than they are now." (SEAN, AGE 10)

"They are near Africas too. It's all close together. They could all go on a safari and try to shoot animals and not the other people." (BRET, AGE 12)

"Iraq is the troublemaker there. But they aren't the only ones. It isn't really our business, but we just hate it when people are violent . . . so we just got to teach them a lesson." (CHANDRA, AGE 9)

"I think Christians should step in and take all of the land. They would rule it better. Besides, it is the Holy Land. There should be no war there."
(FAITH, AGE 13)

"Iran is the worst. But the Iotolla is dead, so they may get less weird. Anything would be an improvement!" (MARVIN, AGE 10)

"I went to Israel with my parents. It was neat. It makes me sad about all the war. I wish they would straighten it all out, so that everybody had the same amount of land and camels."

(RICHARD, AGE 11)

"I read about what happened to the marines in Lebanon. That was terrible. But we have to send spies wherever we can. Next time they should go undercover and wear hoods, so they will fit in better."

(LYNN, AGE 11)

4. The Homeless in America

"We should build one big, gigantic house for all the homeless and make sure it's heated and air-conditioned." (MARVIN, AGE 10)

"You should call the number on TV that tells you how to help them." (GLORIE, AGE 10)

"It makes me unhappy to talk about. I feel sad when I see the holes in their coats." (JAN, AGE 9)

"Give them money if you can afford it. . . . But sometimes they aren't so nice either, and I would be afraid to go near them. Plus their smell is not so good, but they are human beings, too."

(STACEY, AGE 9)

"Were there homeless people at the time of the Revolutionary War?" (MARLENE, AGE 12)

"If they don't like to stay in one place, the government should give them motor homes."

(LIZA, AGE 8)

"I will ask Jesus to help them."

(CHRISTINA, AGE 10)

"It makes me sad. I feel kind of helpless about how to help them. Isn't there more money?"

(ALLIE, AGE 11)

"It is a bad problem. Sometimes they look so hungry and the worse thing of all is that when they do get money, they're stuck eating at McDonald's!"

(LANCE, AGE 12)

"Nobody should be without a house. It ain't right."

(LUKE, AGE 9)

"They should sell things on the street like lemonade and hot dogs in order to make money."

(ROGER T., AGE 11)

"I met a homeless man once at our church. He was really very polite. He even made me laugh. We should help people like him. Maybe it might turn out that we could be in their place, having to beg for food. We wouldn't like it either." (EVIE, AGE 9)

5. Terrorism in the World

"It's a battle to the end for sure!"

(VINCENT, AGE 9)

"We should kidnap all the terror and lock it up."
(BARRIE, AGE 8)

"They have no right to take our hostages! The hostages were ours and they just went out and took them. They should give them all back!"
(AMY, AGE 11)

"I think it's better now. The terrorists found out that they were stupid. Everybody in the whole world says so." (HARLEY, AGE 10)

"Put them behind bars for the rest of their lives and throw away the key. They could just have water and pita bread." (MARINA, AGE 12)

"I wish that we had a real Batman to get the terrorists in Lebanon." (JAMIE, AGE 9)

"I had a nightmare once about tanned men taking over a plane I was flying on. It was scary. I'm against them." (KAREN, AGE 8)

"It's terrible. The cities are not safe. And we need to help other countries that have the same problem."
(MELANIE, AGE 9)

"Terrorism? Yeah, I like those kind of scary movies where the actors are dead." (KATE R., AGE 7)

"It is all the fault of Iran. They sponsor the crazy ones by giving them guns and money and advertisements." (LYLE, AGE 11)

6. The Drug Problem

"They should shut down every store where drugs are sold." (JOHN, AGE 8)

"I would put all the drug pushers in a tub of Jell-O and keep them there!" (SEAN, AGE 10)

"It stinks!" (GLENN, AGE 13)

"They should make jobs for the pushers. It could work if they pay them overtime."
(WALTER, AGE 10)

"I would never do drugs because it might mess up my baseball career." (BRYN, AGE 9)

"They're all bad . . . the people who sell drugs. They are the problem. But some are just sad and depressed. I don't understand why we can't just change things." (MARVIN, AGE 10)

"Just say no! And if that doesn't work, kids should find something else to do, like eating candy or popcorn." (CORY H., AGE 8)

"It's the number one problem in America, and that's no joke at all." (MAURICE, AGE 11)

"We have to stop all the shipments from places like Columbus and all the other places where they make drugs." (BARBARA, AGE 10)

"President Bush should get to understand the problems better. Otherwise he'll be a dope about dope!"
(DANNY, AGE 12)

"Crack is the biggest thing now. . . . Trouble is that there's so much money in it, people don't want to let go." (CHERI, AGE 11)

"Drugs are everything now. I don't know if we will ever stop it. Still, I think we really could if we really wanted to." (KRIS, AGE 13)

"They should have Spuds Mackenzie doing commercials against drugs, instead of beer commercials."
(JANICE R., AGE 9)

7. The State of the Environment

"Clean the whole thing out and start over again."
(JOANNE, AGE 7)

"Which state do you mean? California is a good one, but it may be full of dirt and beaches already!"
(CHUCKIE, AGE 9)

"I like to breathe the air!" (RUTHIE, AGE 6)

"I think we should keep the forests just as they are. We need a lot of green around, and wild things, too. If we knocked out the forests, we would be animals, too!" (SUE, AGE 12)

"Cars are no good for the environment. We should have less of them or else make them more like bikes." (JIMMY, AGE 9)

"I worry about all the fish who have to swim in sewers and the rivers. We ought to be nice to them even if we have to eat them later on."
(SEAN, AGE 10)

"I wonder if other countries have the same troubles we have. Maybe we should ask them. Like in Sweden. Or in Switzerland. How do they keep the land clean?" (EDDIE B., AGE 11)

"The wildlife must be protected! Plus hunters must not shoot them. They are mean and only out for a good, mean time. They should promise not to kill and only use their guns in their own backyards and houses." (TAMARA, AGE 12)

"Pretty soon the whole ocean won't be safe. I like to water-ski, but I may not be able to when I get older. It makes me mad. I think I am going to write to the President about this. Maybe he likes to water-ski, too." (CURTIS, AGE 11)

8. About Oil Spills (accidental or on purpose)

"I felt like crying when I saw those sad birds near where they spilled the oil. Why can't they be more careful. It shows how war is bad for everything around." (SANDRA M., AGE 7)

"That Saddam leader is a nut! Why did he want to spray the oil in the water anyway? Didn't he know he could have sold it? He's a sore loser."

(JASON G., AGE 10)

"It's bad when they spill too much because they don't watch it when they put it in your tank. It makes a mess when you drive into the gas station. It gets on your tires." (BRAD, AGE 10)

"It wasn't the birds' fault. They died because of Mr. Insane." (GEORGE E., AGE 11)

"They better not spill no oil near Cape Cod. We won't be able to go there this summer." (TESS, AGE 8)

"When I saw it on TV, I got mad. People lit it on fire. It could burn up the ocean if they don't get enough firemen." (DANIEL M., AGE 8)

"I think it's disgusting how it gets to the water all black . . . Yeech . . . You have to be a sicko to do that."

(VANCE, AGE 9)

9. Human Rights Violations

"People should be nice to other people. They shouldn't shoot them or hang them."

(MARVIN, AGE 10)

"Other countries should learn from the U.S. Everybody is treated pretty much equal here, except for rich people who have it good."

(MARY JO, AGE 10)

"I am not sure what you mean, but if it's like animal rights like that guy Bob Barker is for, then I'm for it." (TODD, AGE 11)

"There should be an international police department who arrests all the bullies and beats them up till they confess to their crimes."
(ALLYSON, AGE 12)

"The South Americans should be better to their own people. We should teach them about minding their own business!" (LAURIE, AGE 13)

"Like in Russia? Yes, they should have more freedom. What is this glassnoss thing, anyway? Is it some weird jail?" (DANA G., AGE 11)

"Humans are good people." (BO, AGE 6)

"Do on the others what they do for you!"
(LUCY, AGE 7)

"What happened to the students in China was awful. They shot them for nothing. I thought we should have done more. We could have threatened them more. The Russians should have helped, too. The Chinese government is evil. They should be replaced." (LIZ, AGE 13)

"There is still too many dictators in the world . . . like in China. They hurt human beings and even kill them." [HOW CAN WE STOP DICTATORS?] "Right at the beginning, we shouldn't vote for them."
(MAURA, AGE 9)

"It is up to us to make sure everybody has peace and freedom. We should have people in the government in charge of that. President Bush should hire a secretary of peace!" (LEWIS, AGE 11)

10. The United Nations

"Maybe it was what we were called before we were called the 'United States'?" (TESS, AGE 8)

"It's a good idea to have all the countries talk it out. . . . Do you think it will work?"

(ANDREW, AGE 9)

"It was their fault that war started. They should have made peace and stopped the bully stuff."

(CARL, AGE 10)

"They are in New York and they talk into speakers and the speech comes back to them in English . . . but maybe the Arab countries like Iraq don't understand it so good so there is a war."

(MARY ANN T., AGE 10)

"I don't know if they are on our side or somebody else's?" (BETTY, AGE 8)

"I been there. They have some nice flags. Where do they get them? I might like to buy them for my house." (JANE, AGE 8)

"They are sponsors for Halloween. They get kids to go out and collect for them. Mostly money. I don't think they take candy." (BOB M., AGE 13)

★──★

"They are the quiet types from different countries. They aren't the ones who fight the wars. You never see them in uniforms. I don't even know if they got any." (TREVOR, AGE 11)

11. The United States Armed Forces ("The Troops")

"The big general they have is real tough. He is my kind of guy." (PHIL P., AGE 8)

"I like the air people the best. They are very brave and smart. They have to know how to hit the targets so that they don't smash the wrong places—the places that people need . . . Such as a church or maybe a gym." (GEORGE E., AGE 11)

"They are good men and some of the ladies are the best-looking ladies in the whole world."
(BRET, AGE 12)

"I feel bad for their families because it's hard to be away from the ones you love and those stamps cost a ton when you got to get your mail flown over the ocean." (RANDY D., AGE 8)

"I hope they ate good in Saudi Arabia."
(HALLEY, AGE 10)

"They have to eat squishy food. No MacDonald's or nothing over there . . . I don't think I could take it."
(ANDREW, AGE 9)

"Their shirts and pants are neat. But their helmets are kind of useless. They should have facemasks on them, to keep the dust out." (RUSSELL, AGE 10)

"We should be proud of them. They tried to keep the peace but then Iraq started it. Now they are showing them." (STANLEY, AGE 12)

"There are girls who fight in the army and the marines too. That's good. Girls can fight real good. Me and my friends beat up the boys all the time."

(DINA, AGE 8)

12. The Flag and the Pledge of Allegiance

"We got to respect the American flag and its colors. President Bush was right to say nobody should ruin the flag. They shouldn't even iron it!"

(AMY, AGE 11)

"The Pledge to the flag is what we must say every day. But what I don't get is why somebody would burn the flag. They must be upset. We should find out what is wrong instead of letting them go and do it." (GEORGE, AGE 10)

"The Pledge is a good idea. Very good." [WHY?] "Americans should remember their country and it should be first. Otherwise they will forget about America and become Chinese or something."

(TERRY, AGE 10)

"Well, maybe [we should say the Pledge every day]. But I don't think so. What does it prove? It would be

better to sing a patriotic song." [FOR EXAMPLE?]
"Maybe like the 'Star Sprinkled Banner' they sing at
baseball games." (MARGARET U., AGE 10)

"I think we need more than a few minutes for the
Pledge. At least two hours! . . . That way we would
miss both English and Social Studies!"
(KENNY J., AGE 11)

"I feel that if we pledge to the flag, the kids from New
Mexico and places like that might feel left out."
(VANESSA, AGE 8)

"I would be in favor of the Pledge of Legions, but
don't tell my teacher 'cause I don't know the words
so good." (BILLY T., AGE 8)

"It's all good ideas in the Pledge. . . . It's all about
liberty and how we're all the same, even if we have
different houses and different names."
(HOWARD, AGE 8)

13. The Federal Debt

"I don't like the debt, but everybody has a right to
their opinion." (SEAN, AGE 10)

"We could borrow some money from Europe so we
aren't so poor." (JAMILLE, AGE 11)

"The way I look at it, President Bush and Vice President Quayle should give back what they make. That
would probably be an extra million dollars right
there!" (REBECCA, AGE 8)

"The federal death is the number of people who die all over the country. I say we have too many deaths and we have to do something about it."

(LUTHER, AGE 10)

"America should invest in the stock market to make more money." (LORNA, AGE 13)

"Maybe the President could sell one of those marble buildings in Washington. That would help."

(JOHN, AGE 8)

"I have an idea. We could put big stars like Prince and Debbie Gibson on dollar bills so people would want our money more." (GAYLE K., AGE 11)

"I don't see why we don't put our money in one of those ERA accounts my daddy has for his old age."

(REVA, AGE 12)

"We should take a loan from one of those federal saving places." (ANGELO, AGE 11)

"Did you see that movie *Wall Street*? It showed what happens when you care about money too much."

(MIKE F., AGE 10)

"Debt? I never heard of it. Has the President heard of it?" (VAL D., AGE 8)

"I want to know what happens to all the money that people pay to the government!"

(WARREN J., AGE 11)

14. The Space Program

"It's real neat. I like to watch the blast-off and see all the fire burning and the rocket zooming and all the people on the ground acting goofy!"

(STAN, AGE 10)

"I don't understand why they go up when they just come right back down in a few days."

(VERA, AGE 8)

"The *Challenger* thing was sad. I was glad that the *Voyager* was okay. I was afraid that the Russians might try to sabotage it. Or maybe some terrorists might do like they did to the Pan Am plane."

(LLOYD, AGE 10)

"When are they going for a space walk? I heard the astronauts used to. Must have been weird. I want to be an astronaut. I would take a dog with me on one of those walks and see what happens!"

(TERRY, AGE 9)

"I am not in favor of them [shuttle missions]. We should not be trying these trips while we have homeless and poor people. The money should go to them and for people with sickness. Like ones who can't walk or kids who are dying." (WILL, AGE 8)

"We should have more missions with other countries so we can learn about their languages and costumes more." (ALEXIA, AGE 9)

"ZOOM! BOOM! We should go to Mars by next week!" (NATHANIEL, AGE 6)

"The astronauts are very courageous and they deserve a lot of credit. We should hear more about them all the time. They should have more TV shows about them. Like on the Discovery Channel or even on MTV—they could have music videos in space!"

(TERI ANN, AGE 11)

15. The American Educational System

"We should all have a say on the bored of education!"

(MARVIN, AGE 10)

"School is fine . . . especially since we're getting out for the summer in two weeks."

(WINNIE, AGE 10)

"They should have school a half a day all over the country. That would make everybody happy. I bet the teachers wouldn't shout about it either."

(COLIN, AGE 8)

"We need more classes about new history, 'cause a lot is changing right in front of our eyes . . . even if your eyes aren't so old, like mine aren't."

(JAN, AGE 9)

"It's an okay system, but one change I would like to have is for them to get rid of Cs. . . . My dad says I got a few too many already." (TREVOR, AGE 13)

"We need more crayons and different colors here at Reid School. Please, I wish they would send them special delivery to the first grade."

(PAULA, AGE 6)

"They should teach morals instead of math—people wouldn't be so hyper about money then."

(TY, AGE 13)

"President Bush should teach school for a year so he knows what's going on. . . . He might be good at geography or gym." (DALE, AGE 8)

"All this gossip about middle schools is silly. I go to one and it's okay. There's just a lotta kids there, that's all. Maybe people should have less kids."

(MARK, AGE 12)

"I don't see why they need so many principals. What do they do, anyway?" (BRUCE, AGE 11)

"I feel that having to make up snow days is wrong. It's not our fault that it snows. They should take it to the 'People's Court' and let Judge Wapnerd decide." (ANDREA, AGE 10)

"The schools are okay. The parents just aren't concerned enough at home. . . . My parents are different, though. They care." (LAWRENCE F., AGE 10)

"We should have more special classes, on computers and fun stuff like cameras!" (ANDRE, AGE 13)

"I feel they don't teach you enough about life. We learn about what's in books, but not about people and how to get a job and stuff like that. Maybe that's why kids turn to drugs when they get out. The ideas about what's important are all wrong. We need a change." (ROBERTA G., AGE 12)

"School is school. It hasn't changed much since I started a long time ago."
(CARL, AGE 7, SECOND GRADE)

president rooseva

Lou (age 9)

★ *2* ★

"If I Were President, I'd Stay There for a Hundred Years!"

Children Respond to Some Tough Interview Questions

*W*hat would happen if a political interview show were adapted for the six- to thirteen-year-old set? That's what I wondered, so I asked youngsters some challenging interview questions about weighty political matters. After preparing a list of hypothetical presidential situations, I sought the children's counsel. In each case I asked: "What would you do if you were President?"

The resulting political repartee was lively and unpredictable. These interviewees were well prepared for any questions hurled their way, just as men and women at the seat of power must be ready for all political possibilities. While youngsters may not be allowed to stay up for "Nightline," their political skills have not suffered as a consequence!

With apparent ease, the children tackle even the hardest-hitting questions with aplomb and insight. Some youngsters, smitten with politician's fever, adeptly turn the interview format into a forum for their own political ambitions. Others are more philosophical, and choose to expound on the vital social and moral issues of the day.

I was struck by how much the children seem to enjoy these spontaneous conversations. Youngster after youngster displayed great satisfaction during and after the interviews. They like to play at being the President; they enjoy exploring the adult territories of power and responsibility. These boys and girls like to use their imaginations, though their creative responses are also shaped by the real events they read about and hear around them.

But the joy is not one-sided: the children's clever responses are a delight to behold for the adult spectator as well. Their ideas and ambitions make us laugh and take note, for in their comments and views, they touch upon our own views of the Presidency and the land in which we live.

1. Would You Like to Be President?

MICHELLE: "No, I don't think I want to be President."

DH: "How come?"

MICHELLE: "It's no fun."

DH: "How's that?"

MICHELLE: "You have to argue all the time with everybody and you have to sit at your desk and still act cool."

DH: "What's wrong with that?"

MICHELLE: "For one thing, you can't go out and play at all. If you go on the lawn, there's always a helicopter in the way and TV people are always yelling at you."

(INTERVIEW WITH MICHELLE, AGE 8)

LIZ: "If I were President, I'd put a lot of other girls and women in power."

DH: "Why is that?"

LIZ: "The men have not done such a good job. Look at all the wars and the homeless."

DH: "Which jobs would women have?"

LIZ: "Most of them. Giving advice, jobs where you talk to other countries, take care of the country's money, things like this."

DH: "What would you entrust the men with?"

LIZ: "Maybe a man could be the Vice President. They don't say much. I think that some of the boys I know could handle that."

DH: "Any other changes you would make?"

LIZ: "More women in the army as generals and stuff."

DH: "How would that change things?"

LIZ: "We would teach all the troops to sing and dance and be social with other people from other countries."

(INTERVIEW WITH LIZ, AGE 12)

CHARLES: "I already plan to be President."

DH: "Are you sure?"

CHARLES: "Yes, it's going to happen, too. I guarantee it!"

DH: "How do you know?"

CHARLES: "My uncle says I am cut out for it. Because I like to talk a lot and show off."

DH: "What else do you think a President does?"

CHARLES: (pause) "Plans things."

DH: "What kind of things does the President plan, Charles?"

CHARLES: "Mostly plans how he can get elected again and get rid of the other politicians running."

(INTERVIEW WITH CHARLES, AGE 9)

CLIFF: "Let me think about being President and then get back to you."

DH: "Tough question to answer on the spot?"

CLIFF: "No, it's just not something you should do for fun. It's a big job."

DH: "What makes it so big?"

CLIFF: "'Cause if you are no good at it, everybody knows and you get fired after a couple of years."

(INTERVIEW WITH CLIFF, AGE 8)

MALA: "Sure, I'd like to be President. Who wouldn't?"

DH: "Why would you like to be President?"

MALA: "I would like to help people."

DH: "Which people? Anyone in particular?"

MALA: "Yes." (pause) "The ones who voted for me."

(INTERVIEW WITH MALA, AGE 7)

JANINE: "I wouldn't mind being President, but that would be about my third choice."

DH: "Why your third choice?"

JANINE: "There's other things I'd like to do."

DH: "Like what, for example?"

JANINE: "Well, second, I'd like to be a teacher because my mother is a teacher and you get to be with kids and help 'em learn."

DH: "So what would your first choice for a career be?"

JANINE: (giggle) "Well, it sounds silly, but I'd like to be a model and be in *Sports Illustrated.*"

DH: "Why do you think that would be better than being President?"

JANINE: "You get to wear bathing suits all the time. Plus get to travel to places and you aren't stuck in the house all the time."

DH: "But don't Presidents travel a lot?"

JANINE: "Yeah, but that's different. You have to act real conservative all the time. You don't have much freedom."

DH: "I see. . . . So your mind is made up?"

JANINE: "Well, I might be interested in the government when I get older . . . like around sixty. I might either retire with my husband or do something in politics, something easy like be an ambassador to Monte Carlo!"

(INTERVIEW WITH JANINE, AGE 13)

DEAN: "Yes, I would be President, but I need more education first."

DH: "What kind of education would you need?"

DEAN: "I'd need to know all the laws and how to protect them."

DH: "Where do you figure you could get this kind of education? In college? Or somewhere else?

DEAN: "Not in college . . . My brother goes to college, and all he ever does is go to parties and drink beer and go out with blond girls!"

(INTERVIEW WITH DEAN, AGE 10)

ANTHONY: "Could you repeat the question?"

DH: "Would you want to be President?"

ANTHONY: "I don't know."

DH: "Not sure?"

ANTHONY: "Isn't it dangerous?"

DH: "Well, I don't know any Presidents personally."

ANTHONY: "Nah, I'd rather be a fireman. . . . Nobody shoots at you or calls you dirty stuff."

(INTERVIEW WITH ANTHONY, AGE 8)

2. Who Would You Pick as Your Vice President?

CHARLOTTE: "I'd pick Jesse Jackson."

DH: "Why Jesse Jackson?"

CHARLOTTE: "He speaks real good and gets people real excited. . . . If I was President and I made mistakes, at least people wouldn't be mad at me while he was on my side."

(INTERVIEW WITH CHARLOTTE, AGE 9)

SHEILA: "I would pick Kevin on 'The Wonder Years' television show."

DH: "Why would you pick him in particular?"

SHEILA: "He's cute. My mother says he has dimples."

DH: "What does having dimples have to do with being Vice President?"

SHEILA: "Everyone will say he's cute and they will want to vote for him. . . . Unless he looks different close up."

DH: "What do you mean?"

SHEILA: "Like if he has pimples in real life, then that would change everything. . . . I'd have to find somebody new."

(CONVERSATION WITH SHEILA, AGE 8)

RICHARD: "I'd go with someone like Tom Brokaw for Vice President."

DH: "Why would you choose Tom Brokaw?"

RICHARD: "Because he is on TV all the time and it would be good for public relations.

DH: "But wouldn't that be a conflict of interest, since he would be doing the 'NBC Nightly News' and running for Vice President at the same time?"

RICHARD: "If anyone was ticked off, maybe Tom Brokaw would be willing to switch to cable!"

(INTERVIEW WITH RICHARD, AGE 12)

SCOTT: "I would pick a good president of vice."

DH: "Oh, you would, huh? Who might that be?"

SCOTT: "It would be my father for sure. He knows about stuff like that."

(INTERVIEW WITH SCOTT, AGE 6)

CARMEN: "Vice President? Can I pick a kid my age?"

DH: "Sure. It's up to you."

CARMEN: "Then I would pick Ernie Albright."

DH: "Who is Ernie Albright?"

CARMEN: "He's a kid who lives on my block. He's real smart."

DH: "Why would you pick Ernie?"

CARMEN: "He's good with arithmetic."

DH: "How would that be helpful?"

CARMEN: "He could multiply and divide the people's money faster and figure out exactly how much we have."

(INTERVIEW WITH CARMEN, AGE 8)

CHIP: "I think maybe I would pick Ronald Reagan for Vice President."

DH: "But he's already been President."

CHIP: "That's why I'd pick him. He has a lot of experience."

DH: "I guess that's true, but do you think he'd take the job if you offered it to him?"

CHIP: "Yes. I would pay him a big allowance and I bet he's itching to get back in there."

(INTERVIEW WITH CHIP, AGE 8)

JOANNE: "I'd stay with Mr. Quayle as my choice for Vice President."

DH: "You feel he's good for the job."

JOANNE: "No, not really. He's a little young, but so am I. I figure that I could get along with him real good."

DH: "Getting along would seem to be important.

But, Joanne, you aren't afraid of being inexperienced, are you?"

JOANNE: (said with a touch of defiance) "Well, I probably have as much experience as you do! Besides, you must be very busy writing books. But I would be free to be the President twenty-four hours a day!"

(INTERVIEW WITH JOANNE, AGE 12)

MARVIN: "I'd pick the champ, Mike Tyson."

DH: "Why?"

MARVIN: "Because he's cool."

DH: "Any other reason?"

MARVIN: "He'd be a real enforcer. I'd put him in charge of the FBI and nobody would do drugs because they'd be scared of him."

(INTERVIEW WITH MARVIN, AGE 10)

TIM: "I'd pick my mother, Barbara J. Thompson."

DH: "Why would you pick your mother, Tim?"

TIM: "She's nice."

DH: "Any other reasons?"

TIM: "Well, she's good with big problems and plus I couldn't be President unless she was Vice President."

DH: "Why is that, Tim?"

TIM: "Because if she wasn't there, then I'd have to travel all the way back home for dinner or else I'd starve."

(INTERVIEW WITH TIM, AGE 8)

3. What Would Your Campaign Slogan Be?

MICHAEL: "I'M FOR YOU AND THE FOURTH OF JULY!"
DH: "How would you back up that claim?"
MICHAEL: "Wouldn't have to. . . . People always go crazy for those mushy sayings."

(INTERVIEW WITH MICHAEL, AGE 11)

ABBY: "I would promise every girl a dollhouse and every boy a football!"
DH: "But how would that help, since boys and girls don't get to vote?"
ABBY: "They don't?"
DH: "I'm afraid not."
ABBY: "Then they could bug their parents, and their parents could vote for me."

(INTERVIEW WITH ABBY, AGE 9)

MARVIN: "A VOTE FOR MARVIN IS A VOTE FOR FAIRNESS!"
DH: "What do you mean by fairness, Marvin?"
MARVIN: "Everybody is equal."
DH: "How would you put that into practice?"
MARVIN: "Simple . . . Vote for me and they'll see."

(INTERVIEW WITH MARVIN, AGE 10)

EVELYN: "I would tell the citizens of the United States, 'I WILL SET YOU FREE!'"
DH: "Free from what, Evelyn?"
EVELYN: "They will like me."
DH: "Yes, but free from what?"
EVELYN: "Taxes."
DH: "Oh, I see."

(INTERVIEW WITH EVELYN, AGE 10)

CARIN: "CARIN BARNES FOR PRESIDENT!"

DH: "But don't you want to tell the voters what you stand for?"

CARIN: "But I would put that later."

DH: "And what do you stand for?"

CARIN: "I haven't exactly figured that out yet. But when people ask, I'll have an answer."

DH: "Do you think that it might hurt your candidacy not to have an established point of view?"

CARIN: "No, people aren't interested in boring stuff anyway. Besides, I could come up with something if it was a real election."

(INTERVIEW WITH CARIN, AGE 9)

DONALD: "My slogan would be 'PEACE WITH RUSSIA.'"

DH: "I think that might be very popular."

DONALD: "Thanks. I got to work on it still. If you let me have some time, I can come up with something that rhymes."

(INTERVIEW WITH DONALD, AGE 12)

CAROLINE: "SILLY PERSONS SHOULDN'T BE PRESIDENT!"

(INTERVIEW WITH CAROLINE, AGE 7)

MARIO: "MARIO FOR PRESIDENT . . . GEORGE BUSH FOR VICE PRESIDENT . . . MY BROTHER ANTHONY FOR TREASURER!"

DH: "How old is Anthony?"

MARIO: "Five . . . but George and me could help him count."

(INTERVIEW WITH MARIO, AGE 8)

VICKIE: "What kind of slogan am I supposed to pick?"

DH: "Something that sums up your candidacy."

VICKIE: (pause) "I guess it might be something like 'NO MORE ACID RAIN, WHATEVER THAT IS!'"

(INTERVIEW WITH VICKIE, AGE 12)

CHARLIE: "BUSH AND QUAYLE ARE FOR THE BIRDS!"

DH: "Oh, so you are planning on running against the incumbents?"

CHARLIE: "No, just the Republicans!"

(INTERVIEW WITH CHARLIE, AGE 11)

ELLIS: "My slogan would be 'A STRONG ARMY MEANS NO WAR!'"

DH: "That's a very clear slogan. Who do you think will support you?"

ELLIS: "Every red-blooded American!"

DH: "How would you describe those who don't support you?"

ELLIS: "Losers. But they have a right to be losers. It's a free country."

DH: "How would define a loser?"

ELLIS: "You know one when you see one. I wouldn't be mean, though. It's not their fault that they learned to be cowards."

(INTERVIEW WITH ELLIS, AGE 11)

MELANIE: "LOVE EVERYBODY."

DH: "That's a nice idea. Do you think it will be hard for people to follow, Melanie?"

MELANIE: "It shouldn't be. It's only two words."

(INTERVIEW WITH MELANIE, AGE 8)

JAMES: It would be something like 'PUT A MAN IN THE WHITE HOUSE!' "

DH: "Do you think that women might find that slogan a bit sexist?"

JAMES: "What's sexist?"

DH: "Would they be offended by the fact that you are stressing that a man should be in the White House?"

JAMES: "Maybe . . . but they wouldn't want a wimp to be President, would they?"

> (INTERVIEW WITH JAMES, AGE 9)

YVETTE: "FREE MONEY TO EVERYBODY . . . EVEN THE RICH PEOPLE!"

> (INTERVIEW WITH YVETTE, AGE 10)

RAY: "STAMP OUT DRUGS AND PUSH THE PUSHERS INTO THE WOODS WHERE THEY CAN DO DRUGS WITH THE SKUNKS!"

> (INTERVIEW WITH RAY, AGE 12)

4. If You Were Elected President, What Is the First Thing You Would Do?

CHARLENE: "If I was the President, I'd have them plant more flowers."

DH: "What kind of flowers?"

CHARLENE: "Roses and violets and tangerines and mangoes."

DH: "I think that tangerines and mangoes are fruits, not flowers."

CHARLENE: "That's all right. . . . When I'm

President, I am not going to have discrimination against them just 'cause they're different!"

(INTERVIEW WITH CHARLENE, AGE 8)

ARTIE: "The first thing I would do is to deal with the drugs."

DH: "What would you propose to do?"

ARTIE: "Get rid of them."

DH: "How would you do that?"

ARTIE: "Figure something out . . . like a plan."

DH: "What kind of plan?"

ARTIE: "Maybe we could sell all the drugs to Russia real cheap. That would take care of it."

(INTERVIEW WITH ARTIE, AGE 7)

ADAM: "I would buy a lot of toys for all the kids who don't have them."

DH: "That's very kind of you, Adam. How would you pay for all those toys? After all, you might need thousands and thousands of toys."

ADAM: "I'd ask my mother and father for the money."

(INTERVIEW WITH ADAM, AGE 6)

MARVIN: "If I was to be the President, I'd move right up to the White House and relax on a big chair and smoke a big cigar and take it real easy—while everybody else in America worked!"

(INTERVIEW WITH MARVIN, AGE 10)

ANGELA: "I would give the homeless some beds."

DH: "Would you make sure they had a roof over their heads, too?"

ANGELA: "Some of them might like it outside in the summer."

DH: "Maybe, but what about in the winter?"

ANGELA: "I would have to take it one time of year at a time."

(INTERVIEW WITH ANGELA, AGE 9)

TRISHA: "If I were the President, I would hire a national choir like we have at church."

DH: "What would you have them sing about?"

TRISHA: "About peace and love and patriotic songs, too."

DH: "What songs would be your favorite?"

TRISHA: "Oh, I don't know . . . Anything that Bon Jovi and Tiffany do."

(INTERVIEW WITH TRISHA, AGE 11)

SHEENA: "I would get rid of having a President and make the government fair and democratic."

DH: "You don't feel it's democratic now?"

SHEENA: "No."

DH: "What would you do different?"

SHEENA: "I'd make sure that anybody could run for an office, not just people who know people."

DH: "I see, you want your politics to be a more open process."

SHEENA: "Yeah, that's not a bad way to put it. . . . Maybe there could be a job for you on my President's staff!"

(INTERVIEW WITH SHEENA, AGE 9)

MAURA: "I would clean all the air and the water."

DH: "How would you do that?"

MAURA: "With a gigantic vacuum cleaner . . . I

might need to use something else for the big states."

(INTERVIEW WITH MAURA, AGE 7)

FRANK: "If I was elected to be President, I wouldn't change much. But I would make sure everybody respected the flag."

DH: "How would you make sure of that?"

FRANK: "I'd have a Flag Patrol in every town to keep an eye on things."

DH: "Who would be in the Flag Patrol?"

FRANK: "Mostly kids who have nothing to do for the summer."

(INTERVIEW WITH FRANK, AGE 9)

DUANE: "First thing I would do is throw a big party! BYOB! And then I'd invite the whole country!"

(INTERVIEW WITH DUANE, AGE 12)

RAFAEL: "As President of America, I would stand for law and order."

DH: "How would you do that?"

RAFAEL: "What do you mean?"

DH: "I mean what in particular would you do to illustrate that you stand for law and order?"

RAFAEL: "Nothin' . . . I would just stand for it and people would listen."

(INTERVIEW WITH RAFAEL, AGE 9)

DENISE: "The first thing to do is to get a psychiatrist."

DH: "For yourself as President? Why would you get a psychiatrist?"

DENISE: "Because the whole world is crazy!"

(INTERVIEW WITH DENISE, AGE 13)

BOB B.: "If I were President, I'd stay there for a hundred years!"

DH: "Why is that, Bob?"

BOB B.: "Because I would like to meet people from different countries and I would like to have a nice big house, too."

(INTERVIEW WITH BOB B., AGE 10)

5. If You Were President, What Things Would You Be For?

CLIFF: "I would be for peace."

DH: "That's good.... But is anyone against peace?"

CLIFF: "There must be since we don't have much of it!"

(INTERVIEW WITH CLIFF, AGE 8)

MARVIN: "I am for better jobs with better paychecks."

DH: "Hasn't someone used that phrase before?"

MARVIN: "Who?"

DH: "I think maybe a number of people."

MARVIN: "Well, they didn't mean it the way I do."

DH: "How do you mean it?"

MARVIN: "Different . . . I would stop all the hard factory jobs and the ones at construction places. . . . Now, tell me that ain't original."

(INTERVIEW WITH MARVIN, AGE 10)

RONA: "I would be for women's rights."

DH: "Any particular rights you have in mind?"

RONA: "The right to work but not do all the housework."

DH: "Might be a hard thing to legislate."

RONA: "Maybe, but I would try really hard."

DH: "How would you get men to agree?"

RONA: "I would appeal to common sense."

DH: "How would you do that?"

RONA: "Do something that will get their attention . . . Like take sports off the television."

(INTERVIEW WITH RONA, AGE 10)

DEAN: "I would want to improve the way we get along with other places."

DH: "How would you propose to do that?"

DEAN: "I'm not sure."

DH: "Wouldn't that be kind of hard to campaign on? What would you tell the American people?"

DEAN: "With all the political people who are in office now who don't know for sure, why would that be hard?"

DH: "What other places did you have in mind?"

DEAN: "Like China, for one . . . There's too much of a wall between them and us."

(INTERVIEW WITH DEAN, AGE 10)

JULIE: "Hmm . . . I don't know. Maybe for more taxes."

DH: "But don't you think that people would complain about that?"

JULIE: "They should understand it's what a President does. . . . Besides, they don't know what's for their own good!"

(INTERVIEW WITH JULIE, AGE 9)

6. What Would You Be Against?

MITCH: "I'd be against guns."

DH: "Why?"

MITCH: "Because they hurt people and they make people scared."

DH: "Some of the people who disagree with you say that a person has a right to protect himself."

MITCH: "Well, they can say that, but they shouldn't have guns. Or knives either."

DH: "Is there anything they should have?"

MITCH: "Yeah . . . their heads checked!"

(INTERVIEW WITH MITCH, AGE 12)

TINA: "Against? I wouldn't want to be against anything."

DH: "Surely there must be something you'd be against, Tina."

TINA: "No, then nobody would like me."

DH: "But what if they were against the same things you are?"

TINA: "I'll have to think about it. . . . I still don't think that people like a President who is against things."

(INTERVIEW WITH TINA, AGE 8)

LEN: "I am most against dentists."

DH: "Dentists? How come?"

LEN: "Because they drill you all the way through your mouth."

DH: "But does a President have authority over a dentist? I don't think most dentists are connected to the government."

LEN: "Presidents ought to. Dentists are always

weird. And they hate kids. If I was President, I would make it a law that you couldn't be a dentist unless you passed a special test."

DH: "What kind of test?"

LEN: "A hard one . . . so no one would pass."

DH: "But then there wouldn't be any dentists."

LEN: "That's right. . . . You got it now."

DH: "Been to the dentist lately, Len?"

LEN: "Yesterday . . . but I don't want to talk about it!"

(INTERVIEW WITH LEN, AGE 9)

MARTHA: "I would definitely be against men being at the top of all the businesses."

DH: "How would you change things?"

MARTHA: "Make a law that half the people have to be women."

DH: "Do you think that businesses would cooperate?"

MARTHA: After a while, they would realize that it's only a matter of time before they have to say 'uncle.'"

(INTERVIEW WITH MARTHA, AGE 13)

RANDALL: "I'd be against pushy people like the ones in the Senate!"

(INTERVIEW WITH RANDALL, AGE 10)

CLIFF: "I would be opposed to war, especially the ones where you can't see the enemy. Those are very bad."

(INTERVIEW WITH CLIFF, AGE 8)

JANINE: "I am against smoking and feel they should outlaw the tobacco makers. . . . It's just another form of drugs, but they don't want to change it 'cause the smokers would cough in their faces if they did."

(INTERVIEW WITH JANINE, AGE 13)

SIMON: "I'm against work—just like Garfield!"

(INTERVIEW WITH SIMON, AGE 9)

LUIS: "I am definitely not in favor of prejudice. Bigots just like to shoot their mouths off 'cause they have nothin' else to shoot!"

(INTERVIEW WITH LUIS, AGE 8)

CHARLOTTE: "I'm not against much . . . just school!"

(INTERVIEW WITH CHARLOTTE, AGE 9)

7. What Would You Do to Help Our Relations with Other Countries?

LEIGH ANN: "I would send letters to all the other countries on purple paper."

DH: "Why on purple paper?"

LEIGH ANN: "Because everybody likes purple. . . . It makes you feel happy."

DH: "What would you say in the letters?"

LEIGH ANN: "That they should write me back on purple paper."

DH: "And how would this help?"

LEIGH ANN: "Through all the writing, we could understand each other better . . . and see that we have a lot the same."

DH: "Like purple paper?"

LEIGH ANN: Yes. But pink would be okay, too. We shouldn't try to dictate to them!"

(INTERVIEW WITH LEIGH ANN, AGE 8)

BRANDI: "I believe that we are already doing everything we can to help them."

DH: "But I was wondering about how we could improve relations with them."

BRANDI: "Relations are a bad idea."

DH: "Why?"

BRANDI: "I mean our President shouldn't have no romance with a foreign person, like a French person or a Russian!"

(INTERVIEW WITH BRANDI, AGE 9)

WILL: "Be friends with them and give them a handshake."

DH: "But what if they are too far away for a handshake? How can we communicate with other countries?"

WILL: "Put the handshake on film and send them a movie."

(INTERVIEW WITH WILL, AGE 8)

IRV: "With China I would tell them they are wrong and no good to their people."

DH: "Do you feel that would help our relations with them?"

IRV: "I think so. . . . The people there will like us better for it. They will probably want to come to America. Here's it's okay to have rebellion against the government. We don't mind. . . . But it's backward there."

(INTERVIEW WITH IRV, AGE 10)

CAMILLE: "I would say we shouldn't put our nose in where it doesn't belong."

DH: "Can you give me an example?"

CAMILLE: "Well, like in Central America."

DH: "Do you mean Nicaragua?"

CAMILLE: "Yes."

DH: "Some people feel that it is a threat to us— because the government there is Communist-influenced."

CAMILLE: "That's different. I didn't know that. Maybe it's all right if we get a little involved."

(INTERVIEW WITH CAMILLE, AGE 13)

MARVIN: "We should send more food and supplies to Africa."

DH: "You mean for humanitarian reasons?"

MARVIN: "What's human-tarian reasons?"

DH: "Just that we offer to give free help to people to show that we care about their welfare."

MARVIN: "Who said anything about *free* supplies!"

(INTERVIEW WITH MARVIN, AGE 10)

MARSHALL: "Let's make the world one big country so there are no more differences."

(INTERVIEW WITH MARSHALL, AGE 12)

EMMITT: "We should have more meetings with all the countries."

DH: "You mean like at the United Nations?"

EMMITT: "No, we should really have talks with the leaders. Like with President Reagan and King Gorbachev."

DH: "I don't think Gorbachev's title is king."

EMMITT: "Then we shouldn't waste time with him.

We should talk straight with who is in charge!"
(INTERVIEW WITH EMMITT, AGE 7)

8. What Changes Would You Make Here in America?

HECTOR: "Nothing. I like it the way it is."
DH: "Hector, you mean there's nothing at all that you would like to change?"
HECTOR: "No . . . nothing that I can think of . . . Well, maybe just the President."
(INTERVIEW WITH HECTOR, AGE 11)

JUSTINE: "I think the planes should be safer. There's too many crashes."
DH: "What would you do as President to improve things?"
JUSTINE: "They should check them more. Make sure they have seat belts and the wings are okay."
DH: "You seem to be quite knowledgeable about airplanes. Do you fly often?"
JUSTINE: "No, I never been on one. . . . But I can dream."
(INTERVIEW WITH JUSTINE, AGE 9)

ANN MARIE: "I would like to make summer longer."
DH: "That would be a hard thing to change. I don't think the President can control how long summer is."
ANN MARIE: "No . . . God does that. . . . But if I was President, I could change when school begins. I would move it till at least October."
(INTERVIEW WITH ANN MARIE, AGE 8)

TOM: "Everything."

DH: "You would try to change everything if you were President?"

TOM: "Yes."

DH: "Wouldn't it be difficult to be elected if you wanted to change *everything?*"

TOM: "I wouldn't tell anybody before the election."

DH: "But wouldn't the citizens get upset if you tried to change everything?"

TOM: "Well, I'd have to change their minds, too."

(INTERVIEW WITH TOM, AGE 13)

DANA: "Maybe we should be more loyal to America."

DH: "What do you mean by loyal, Dana?"

DANA: "People should love America and care about it all the time."

DH: "How can citizens best demonstrate their love?"

DANA: "They can start by not throwing their garbage all over the place . . . on the street . . . in the harbor . . . in front of the stores."

DH: "Where is litter the worst, Dana?"

DANA: "Probably in my sister Pam's room. She's a real pig!"

(INTERVIEW WITH DANA, AGE 8)

SMITTY: "I would make people pay attention when they are facing the flag and singing the national anthem at baseball games."

DH: "You don't feel people pay enough attention?"

SMITTY: "Haven't you ever seen? They're too busy drinking and acting like jerks!"

DH: "What could you do to change that?"

SMITTY: "Hit a hardball at them when they aren't looking!"

(INTERVIEW WITH SMITTY, AGE 10)

PEGGY: "If I were Ms. President, I would be on television every night so all the voters could keep a close eye on me. That would be a big change!"

(INTERVIEW WITH PEGGY, AGE 9)

JAY: "I would add some others along with the Republicans and Democrats. . . . It gets pretty dull with just the two of them."

(INTERVIEW WITH JAY, AGE 10)

MELANIE: "I would keep the Christmas tree at the White House for the whole year. . . . That way maybe we would have more peace."

(INTERVIEW WITH MELANIE, AGE 8)

9. If You Were the President, What Would You Do Especially for Kids?

PHILLIP: "Kids would want things like bubble gum machines in the schools."

DH: "Would you try to arrange for it if you were President?"

PHILLIP: "Sure . . . Why not?"

DH: "I can't see any reason."

PHILLIP: "You'd have to put in a dollar, though . . . and the money would go for good causes."

DH: "For example?"

PHILLIP: "Like helping sick kids and ones without

parents and ones who have hungers. . . . That's what a President is for!"

(INTERVIEW WITH PHILLIP, AGE 9)

JILLIAN: "For kids? I would teach them more about our country, about the Revolutionary War and all. But for twelve-year-olds, I would give us more rights so we can be recognized more like older people."

DH: "Don't you think you might get some complaints from eleven-year-olds who want to be included in?"

JILLIAN: "What? Have them vote, too? . . . Jeezus, you have to draw the line somewheres!"

(INTERVIEW WITH JILLIAN, AGE 12)

JUAN: "Kids need more property to play on."

DH: "So you would like to create more playgrounds and playing fields?"

JUAN: "Yeah, I would keep the places like Yankee Stadium and Shea Stadium, where the Mets are, open all the time for the kids to play on . . . so long as they don't mess up the grass."

(INTERVIEW WITH JUAN, AGE 8)

DIANA: "Nuthin' . . . A President is a grown-up. He does things for grown-ups."

(INTERVIEW WITH DIANA, AGE 6)

GRANT: "They should have a TV show about the President and the news events that are happening for kids. That would be a good idea."

DH: "Do you feel this would be educational?"

GRANT: "Probably . . . Maybe the President and Dan Quayle could answer kids' questions, too."

DH: "Oh, a news conference. What kind of questions do you think kids would ask?"

GRANT: "Smart ones . . . not the dumb ones that the TV people do!"

(INTERVIEW WITH GRANT, AGE 10)

JOHNNY: "I would have more kids over the White House building and let them play Double Dragon Nintendo there!"

(INTERVIEW WITH JOHNNY, AGE 7)

KATE: "I would have a Kids' Day. It would be on a Monday like all the other holidays, and people would send cards and have parties."

DH: "What date would you choose?"

KATE: "Not in the summer . . . I want the day off from school! Maybe around May sixth. We usually have a lot of tests then."

(INTERVIEW WITH KATE, AGE 9)

IVAN: "I'd have kids run the whole government. You should be asking what we would have to do with adults, because they would be in the minority. . . . I'd be a nice guy and I'd be easy on them— even my parents!"

(INTERVIEW WITH IVAN, AGE 12)

10. What Do You Think the President Will Be Like in the Year 2000?

DANIELLE: "Probably a zombie or something like that. Everything will be science fiction then."

(INTERVIEW WITH DANIELLE, AGE 10)

RHONDA: "Maybe a girl."
>> (INTERVIEW WITH RHONDA, AGE 7)

JAYNE: "The President might be someone we never heard of."
DH: "Who, for example?"
JAYNE: "Maybe even you!"
>> (INTERVIEW WITH JAYNE, AGE 11)

BRIAN S.: "It could be Ron Quayle."
DH: "Do you mean Vice President Dan Quayle?"
BRIAN S.: "Yes, but I think probably his name will be the same as it is now. He won't change it."
>> (INTERVIEW WITH BRIAN S., AGE 9)

DENNIS T.: "The President may be from another country by 2000."
DH: "But doesn't the President have to be born in America?"
DENNIS: Oh, then there might not be much different than it is now, except they'll know what the people want before they vote."
DH: "How will that be known?"
DENNIS: "By 2000, they'll have computers that are so awesome, they can read people's minds."
DH: "Will they be able to read the President's mind, too?"
DENNIS: "No, that would be dangerous."
>> (INTERVIEW WITH DENNIS, AGE 12)

DEBBIE: "The President will have to be different, probably smarter. He'll have to speak more languages. Everything will be different then. Even some of the countries."

DH: "What kind of person will the President be?"

DEBBIE: "He'll be nice, too. And he might be black. It could happen by then."

DH: "Who will it be? Could it be Jesse Jackson?"

DEBBIE: "Maybe, but I don't think so. It might be someone from sports. It might be Bo Jackson, except that he will probably want to do another job at the same time."

(INTERVIEW WITH DEBBIE, AGE 9)

EDIE: "President Bush will be real gray by the year 2000. Especially since he will have been the President for so many years. . . . He sure would have a lot of worries by then."

(INTERVIEW WITH EDIE, AGE 9)

CHRISTIAN: "There could be two Presidents by then. One won't be enough for all the people there will be."

DH: "How will the two Presidents divide up their responsibilities?"

CHRISTIAN: "One will take the East and the other one will take the West and they'll have to split up the middle."

(INTERVIEW WITH CHRISTIAN, AGE 10)

DESMOND: "The year 2000! That's a long time from now. The President will be a person the citizens see more. He will have to mix more with the people and not just be on the news."

(INTERVIEW WITH DESMOND, AGE 9)

MARVIN: "The year 2000? It could even be somebody in my class!"

DH: "See any candidates sitting around you?"

MARVIN: "Nah, most of them have too much trouble with math and common sense."

(INTERVIEW WITH MARVIN, AGE 10)

FRANK: "It might be a person like Kemp."

DH: "Do you mean Jack Kemp, the secretary of HUD?"

FRANK: "What's HUD? No, I mean the guy who was running for President. You must be thinking of somebody else."

DH: "No, I think it's the same one."

FRANK: "Can't be."

DH: "Yes, do you know he used to be a quarterback in the NFL?"

FRANK: "No . . . maybe he's not a good choice. He might be too busy already."

(INTERVIEW WITH FRANK, AGE 9)

HOWARD G.: "By 2000, it will be some person who is real famous. . . . But they'll be weird-looking by then, too."

DH: "What would the President look like?"

HOWARD G.: "Weird . . . something like Alf."

(INTERVIEW WITH HOWARD G., AGE 8)

ELAINE: "In 2000, we will celebrate a lot . . . the whole year. The President will have to be a man or woman who is fun."

DH: "Do you mean to suggest that the past and current Presidents are not fun people?"

ELAINE: "No comment!"

(INTERVIEW WITH ELAINE, AGE 11)

Gerold Ford

Karen (age 8)

★ *3* ★

"Uncle Sam Is That Nosy Relative of the President!"

*Children Explain Some Patriotic and
Political Phrases*

*A*s students of American history, children know the importance of understanding patriotic and political terms. An ambiguous communication by a President could cause a war. And in the classroom, such oversights might also lead to a dreadful fate—a failing grade!

Despite their interest in history and politics, sometimes youngsters cannot summon to mind the precise definition of a patriotic or political term. Does that mean that our children are silent when faced with a hard-to-explain phrase? On the contrary, children will offer a creative guess or two about such head-scratchers as "What is an electoral college?" or "What are hawks and doves?" In their very free associations to such terms, youngsters reveal a great deal about how they believe our government works.

Their verbal journeys often reveal what children think about America's role at home and abroad. Spontaneous remarks get at the heart of the children's patriotic zeal. But children's answers are entertaining, too, and they make us take stock of our own political acumen! After all, where do those donkey and elephant symbols come from, anyway?

1. "The Cabinet"

"I'm not sure what it could be. It might be the place they keep all the guns and bombs."

(ELLIS, AGE 11)

"The friends of the President who come over and have a few drinks and talk about current events and the stock market." (JAY, AGE 10)

"The Cabinet is where the Mrs. President hides all her jewelry and clothing for the big events so nobody can see what she is going to wear."

(GLORIA, AGE 7)

"Maybe the Cabinet is a special place in the Senate where they keep things like the Declaration of Independence. There's probably a lot of old things like that in the Cabinet." (KEN, AGE 10)

"It's where they store the food."

(EDITH, AGE 10)

"The *Cabinet* might be the name of the President's boat. You know, like *Air Force One* is his plane. He probably sails it around the Potomac River." (pause) "Except they would call it *Navy One* then. Maybe it's something else." (SHEILA, AGE 10)

"That's kind of a trick one. But I know it. The Cabinet is the people who the President picks to run parts of the government." [WHAT PARTS ARE THERE?] 'Well there's a guy who runs the police, and another who runs the fires, and another who chases you down if you don't cough up your taxes, and one who flies around the country telling you how good the President's doing, and maybe one to keep an eye on all the others." (PAT, AGE 12)

"The Cabinet? That's easy. Ask me a tough one. Like National Security Advisers. Those are the spies that send guns to South America and hook up there with the CIA, so they can give a big surprise to the President. I think Ollie North was an adviser. But there are others now because he was on trial."

(AL, AGE 13)

2. "Hawks and Doves"

"Two kinds of animals found around Washington."

(MARCI, AGE 13)

"They are nicknames for the air force and the navy. They use them for their teams."

(BILL T., AGE 11)

"Dove is a dishwasher soap you buy in the store. What does that have to do with the government?"

(CHERYL, AGE 11)

"A hawk? It could be like what's on the flag in the South. Like in Florida. The hawks fly there for the winter, so they have them on the flag there. I don't know dove, but it might stand for the North."

(KEITH, AGE 9)

"I know that. Hawks and doves are either for war or for peace. The doves are cowards. Every year the hawks and doves get together and shout at each other like at a football game. They might even do the wave. But the doves always get smooshed because they are afraid to fight. Still, there are always a few doves who come back a year after to yell and get smooshed again!" (HARRY, AGE 12)

"They are different breeds or species. Like humans and monkeys are from the same species. Well, hawks and doves are a different one totally."

(SELINA, AGE 11)

3. The Department of Defense and the Pentagon

"The military people who give the orders to invade places like Vietnam and Panama and Kuwait. . . . They don't invade Russia even if we don't like them because we don't need a nuclear war."

(HELEN, AGE 13)

"A pentagon is one of those shapes, but I always get it wrong on the shape test." (ALEX, AGE 11)

"They might be the people you call when you want to build a fence around you because the dogs are all coming into your yard from down the block."

(CHANDRA, AGE 9)

"They are on television all the time now. They tell you what we did and what Iraq does and what Russia is doing. Then they tell you who is winning. They are kind of like the broadcasters." (VANCE, AGE 9)

"They are scud-busters!" (BOB M., AGE 13)

"Maybe it's the people who *defend* whatever the President says. They show you that he's no liar and he tries as hard as he can." (MELANIE, AGE 9)

"I don't know exactly what a Pentagon is . . . It sounds like tent. Do they sell tents there?"

(DON, AGE 8)

"The Defense is the part of the government that makes our weapons, like bombs and guns. The people like my dad have to pay for it, though. That's why they pay taxes. . . . That's why we can't pay for a new car." (JASON G., AGE 10)

"That's where all the generals play with the miniature tanks and yell: 'GOTCHA.'"

(DAVID S., AGE 11)

"They might be advisors to the President and the Vice President. They tell them when they need money, which is quite a lot of the time."

(MARK P., AGE 10)

4. "The Hill"

"It's a big mountain that's tough to climb."
(MICHAEL, AGE 10)

"The Hill is a place in the President's backyard.
. . . He hits golf balls from there and practices his golf
swings. . . . It's far enough away so he doesn't break
any windows." (REID, AGE 10)

"They have rides and toys there, and at Christmas,
Santa Claus comes and you can see him."
(MELANIE, AGE 6)

"The Hill is in Fairfield (Connecticut). It's where all
the rich people live." (MARVIN, AGE 10)

"It's the porch where the President lives. He goes out
there to take out the garbage, or probably he has
someone take it out for him. . . . The Secret Service
would be mad if he went out alone."
(JAN, AGE 11)

"The big towers in Washington where they all gossip
about the country." (JAY, AGE 10)

"The Hill? Who cares?" (GEORGE, AGE 10)

"There are a lot of hills all over the place. There's a
hill near where I live. My brother said they used to
go sledding there till they wouldn't let them anymore. That's too bad, because it's real big and it's
good for sledding." (GLORIA, AGE 7)

5. "Veto"

"It's what the President does when he doesn't like a law. He puts a line through what he doesn't like, and then it's all changed. They don't do this too much since people would complain." (PAT, AGE 12)

"The name of a big dog. His name is Vito."
(JOHN, AGE 9)

"It's a planet real far away. You probably can't see it from here. Maybe they are thinking of sending a satellite there. It would be without men."
(JAMES, AGE 10)

"A job in the government where you collect papers and go through them and keep your mouth shut."
(ALEX, AGE 11)

"It's a strange particle we might have covered in science class." (VAN, AGE 9)

"Veto? It might be a certain kind of vote they take, and if anybody important votes 'no,' then that's the way the vote goes." [ANYBODY IMPORTANT?] "Yeah, but I don't know who it would be. But you can bet it's somebody the others listen to."
(STEVIE, AGE 11)

"A Vito is an Italian person who has tons of power."
(ELISSA, AGE 10)

6. "Patriot"

"They're a football team. They were lousy last year. They only won one game. Plus they got in trouble because they made faces at that *Herald* lady and she didn't like it." (VANCE, AGE 9)

"Those bombs that know how to kill the enemy but they don't kill anybody else. They are programmed to know when there is an American around, so . . . that they . . . stay clear."
(GEORGE E., AGE 11)

"They were the ones that fought the British. They were the main reason we won."
(RUSSELL, AGE 10)

"It was the patriot missiles versus the scuds and the scuds lost. They shoot 'em into the sky and they make fireworks, but not exactly like you see in the harbor during the summer." (BRAD, AGE 10)

"A patriot is anybody who owns a flag. It doesn't matter if you are old or new; you can be a patriot if you like red, white, and blue."
(TREVOR, AGE 11)

"I think it was like Ben Franklin and the people who didn't want to pay for the stamps."
(HALLEY, AGE 10)

"It's a weapon that they used in Saudi. But it's also a name for somebody who loves his country and is willing to say it in front of everybody . . . some of them have hats that say U.S.A. on it."

(ERIC B., AGE 13)

7. "Electoral College"

"It's in Pennsylvania. It's where the President goes to learn about the people. He has to take courses in making speeches and stuff like that."

(CHARLES, AGE 9)

"It might be wherever the President who is in there now went to college. Like Bush. He went to Yale. And Reagan. Where did he go? Do you know? Did he go to college?" (REID, AGE 10)

"I'm not sure. . . . Maybe it's the power company that keeps the lights going in the Capitol Building. Many people take these things for granted, but it is important because all the men and women work late sometimes." (ANDREA, AGE 10)

"I never heard of anything like that. Is it a big school?" (ABBY, AGE 9)

"I've heard of it. It's not like a school or anything." (pause) "Ask a grown-up. They might be able to help you out. It's probably a department or something in the government that makes sure nobody cheats on income tax." (JILL, AGE 11)

"That sounds like a silly thing. . . . Let's draw some more pictures of the Presidents."

(GINA B., AGE 7)

"An electoral college is a group of people who meet in Washington every once in a while. Like the senators." [WHAT DO THEY DO?] "I think that maybe they are in charge of education. They make sure the teachers don't mess up and teach us magic and religion and geometry before we're ready."

(CLAYTON, AGE 10)

"It's how we elect the President after the candidates are through with running all the TV ads about each other." (DREW, AGE 8)

"Could be something to do with elections, like maybe it's the auditorium where they hold the debates to see who is better." (KEITH, AGE 9)

8. "IRS"

"They are the people who take money and things from all the rest of us." [WHAT KIND OF THINGS?] "Like your clothes and your house and your car, too. Anything they are short on."

(MADELEINE, AGE 13)

"It means that 'I REST SOFT' when I am the President." (ELAINE, AGE 10)

"IRS is a big computer that stores all the data on the people and says whether they have been obeying law and paying traffic bills and voting on time."

(OLIVER, AGE 10)

" 'INVEST IN A RAT STATE'—it's probably a heavy metal group that is known about in some

parts of the country. Maybe they do political stuff."
(MILT T., AGE 9)

"It's like the FBI but even more of a secret."
(MARVIN, AGE 10)

"Those are three letters that don't mean anything because there aren't enough vowels in them."
(LAURA ANN, AGE 7)

"IRS is a company in Canada that does business here in America." (GARRY, AGE 9)

"I think that it's the people in the government who collect the taxes. . . . People don't like them for the most part since you never see who they are, but they always keep calling you until you answer them."
(CAROLYN Y., AGE 13)

9. "Domestic Policy"

"I think it's the part of the government that takes care of all the pests that would ruin all the fruits and vegetables." (LOUISE, AGE 9)

"Dum'estic has to do with the people who are stupid. . . . The President has to make sure there is free money for them, otherwise they would be in trouble." (MITCHELL, AGE 8)

"It's a government thing that they announce after it happens—so nobody gets the jump on them."
(OZZIE, AGE 10)

"Domestic is the President's policy on how many foreign people can come and live in America. We would like to give them all freedom, but there's only a small amount of room. . . . We should use the land in Utah and Wyoming more." (CORY, AGE 11)

"Domestic what? I've never heard of it. . . . Oh, yeah . . . It's when the Congress is fed up with the President and so their policy is to try to get rid of him!"
(CARRIE, AGE 11)

"I believe it is the rules about what a President can tell his wife. . . . But nobody really goes by them [the rules]. . . . Look at how the Reagans used to blab about everything and even told an astology person."
(ALEXANDRIA, AGE 12)

"The policy is always to fly the flag high and be proud of the United States and try to help people who need us, like people in floods and hurricanes and wars . . . and also to keep us strong by showing that we don't take crap from terrorists or drug dealers, even if they live right here." (GINO, AGE 12)

"A domestic policy is a plan to give money to the hungry and to give jobs to everybody who wants one . . . and if somebody doesn't want one, it's too bad. But even if they don't want to work, they can still vote. A domestic policy doesn't keep anybody from voting, at least that I know of."
(GLYNNIS, AGE 13)

10. "New World Order"

"Another idea of President Bush's . . . I haven't figured out what it is yet." (STANLEY, AGE 12)

"It could be some alien group they ran into on Star Trek: The Next Generation." (ROSS, AGE 8)

"That's what Columbus was trying to do . . . He was looking for the new world." (RYAN, AGE 11)

"It is the idea that everybody should get along and have peace. It's not like that now. There's too much war. But it could be like that in ten years."
(MYRA, AGE 13)

"Maybe because there's too much terrorism around, they need more law and order."
(BARBARA Y., AGE 9)

"That could be the name of the new football league that is going to have teams from places like Spain."
(KYLE B., AGE 11)

11. "Chief Justice"

"Warren Burgers . . . His brother Ham is also a lawyer!" (laughter) (JEREMY, AGE 12)

"The part of the police that handles parking tickets." (ELAINE, AGE 10)

"It's when you did a bad crime and they take you to a jail and they bring you to the electric chair and

then they say: 'Here's some justice for you, Chief.' "
                                    (WALTER, AGE 10)

"Chief Justice is a guy in the courts who is supposed
to fix druggies, and I don't mean no people who work
for the CVS drugstores." (ROBERT, AGE 9)

"Chief Justice was one of the Indian leaders we
fought in the West. I think we got him but, it took
a lot of battles and soldiers." (WILL, AGE 9)

"It's the person in the President's advisers who must
be the most brave, because he always has to tell the
President exactly what is going on in the country."
                                    (RENALDO, AGE 10)

"Head of the army. Probably always a man. It figures." (DEBRA B., AGE 11)

12. "Lame Duck"

"A lame duck is a thing in water, underneath the
water, that doesn't need to come up for air."
                                    (J.T., AGE 10)

"Mike Dukakis." (MARCI, AGE 13)

"A duck that is hurt and has no friends."
                                    (JAEL, AGE 8)

"It means a very, very dumb government person."
                                    (MARVIN, AGE 10)

"I'm sure it's not actually an animal. It's a name for
something. Like something all the Congress is
against." (DONALD, AGE 12)

"It might be a code word for something in the military." (TY, AGE 13)

"Lame duck? Boy, that's a thing that nobody's heard. . . . It must be real strange." (PHYLLIS, AGE 9)

"Is that something to do with the President? Is that like when the President goes hunting? I knew he likes to fish, but I didn't know he liked hunting. Maybe he doesn't like to advertise that."
(CARLTON, AGE 13)

13. "Minority Leader"

"The person in the government who makes sure there is no prejudice, and if there is, he tells people to change their ways." (CORY, AGE 11)

"Someone who leads the gym class at school and makes sure you're wearing the right kind of shorts."
(JOHN, AGE 9)

"Leader of the soldiers who are stationed in Washington to protect the President." (LUIS, AGE 8)

"It's what you climb on when you want to paint a house." (FELIX, AGE 9)

"A person like Jesse Jackson who speaks for poor people and minority people." (MIRA, AGE 13)

"I'll give you an example. Michael Jordan leads basketball in scoring, so he is a leader. But he's black and is therefore a minority." (ELLIS, AGE 11)

"It's somebody in the House of Representatives who gets to speak whenever he wants to."

(DOROTHY, AGE 12)

14. "Uncle Sam"

"A nickname for the President . . . Only his friends call him that." (BILL T., AGE 11)

"Uncle Sam is somebody you can count on for advice, like if you're having problems at school. He'll help you get A's and you won't have to worry anymore."

(BRYN, AGE 9)

"I don't have an Uncle Sam, so I don't know what he'd be like. . . . Probably he'd be like my Uncle Phil, who's pretty nice and takes us to the ball games sometimes." (MITCHELL, AGE 7)

"Uncle Sam is that nosy relative of the President that always tries to give him advice about money and foreign relations. The President has to tell him to mind his own business." (ANDY, AGE 9)

"Wasn't he the speaker guy who retired a couple of years ago and then wrote some big bestseller book?"

(PIA, AGE 11)

"He could be one of the heroes in the Revolutionary War—like Nathan Hale and Tom Paine. I'm not sure, but I pictured the Bunker Hill Monument, so maybe that's right." (TIM, AGE 12)

"How do *you* know my uncle? Uncle Sam is a good uncle, but he doesn't have anything to do with the government. He votes, though."

(JESSICA, AGE 9)

"Uncle Sam is a name they use for America. . . . There's no such person; it's like Santa Claus. . . . But he represents a lot, so people talk about him."

(MARK R., AGE 13)

15. "CIA"

"It's what they whisper when they want to say that a CHILD IS ASLEEP." (OLIVE, AGE 8)

"Part of the armed forces of America . . . I'm not sure what they do. . . . Does anybody know?"

(MARVIN, AGE 10)

"CIA . . . It means a 'COMMITTEE IN AMERICA.' . . . It's the committees in the Congress. They do all kinds of things about AIDS and drugs and justice."

(JAMIE, AGE 10)

"They are spies for Russia and Germany who try to sabotage us." (DARNELL, AGE 12)

"A CIA must be something like a special letter from the President, with his name on it."

(ANONYMOUS, AGE 10)

16. "Oval Office"

"It's a room in the White House, but it's not on the people's tour you pay for." (ANDREA, AGE 10)

"It's a place where you go and there's plenty of room so you can play with your yo-yo."

(STEVIE O., AGE 10)

"An oval is a round thing, but a whole person couldn't fit in it." (FAITH, AGE 7)

"The workplace of the President . . . He keeps his paper clips and erasers there." (ANITA, AGE 11)

"It's a strange place." (PHILIPPA, AGE 6)

"The place where the President's wife has her hair done . . . If the President was a girl, she'd have her hair done there, too." (JACKIE, AGE 9)

"Must be the President's office. It might be called oval because he could have a big oval dart board on the wall and he throws darts at the Congress and other people he doesn't like." (SHEILA, AGE 9)

"Where the President does his homework. Well, he doesn't really have homework like we do, but you know what I mean. He has a big desk there and lots of space and a picture of his dog there. He could have a computer, too, so that way he'll get the latest information on the news and the weather. . . . He has to know the weather 'cause he travels so much. . . . Well, there's plenty in his office and sometimes he greets the visitors there, too, like when he's posing for pictures or making a deal with somebody important . . . the usual stuff that a President does to make a living." (NATHAN, AGE 12)

17. "Secretary of State"

"A person in every state who counts all the people and makes sure they stay where they are, and they don't try to sneak over to another state."

(BRYN, AGE 9)

"It will be me—when I grow up and learn how the government works!" (PAUL, AGE 8)

"Usually a lady with nice legs and 'cause they type better." (JAMES, AGE 9)

"The person in the democracy who is like a fireman and makes sure that all the big fires are put out across the land." (SHEILA, AGE 9)

"A big official person who tells the President what to do . . . The President listens so he don't hurt their feelings, but he don't take them too serious."

(VICKIE, AGE 11)

"The President's secretary for personal junk. The secretary answers all his mail, like from foreign people and kids who write to the President, like we are going to." (RONNIE, AGE 8)

"Was it that girl, Fawn Hall?"

(JOANNE, AGE 11)

18. "Operation Desert Storm"

"It sounds like a doctor who operates in places that have a lot of deserts." (LONNIE, AGE 8)

"That's what they call it any time we bomb a country we hate." (VANCE, AGE 9)

"It's the name of the way we went in and fought Saddam Hussein and his men. It happened in the desert. But I didn't know there was big storms there." (RUSSELL, AGE 10)

"It's got something to do with the war. It might be a secret mission for the women in the army. They do special stuff." (MARY ANN T., AGE 10)

"That was the hurricane problems they had down south last year. A bunch of people got their houses wrecked. They were lucky to get out alive."
(BRAD, AGE 10)

"Operation Desert Storm is what George Bush invented so we knew we had a war on our hands."
(STANLEY, AGE 12)

"Maybe it's what the marines and the air force have to do in Saudi Arabia. They have to clean up the desert so it is fit to live in." (BRENT, AGE 10)

19. "Donkeys and Elephants"

"Things that make up the big jungle."
(KYLE, AGE 8)

"They are part of the zoo. . . . Maybe they have a zoo where the President lives." (WILL, AGE 9)

"Those are the political parties. But there are also Independent people, too. I don't know what animal they have. Maybe giraffes, because there aren't that many of them." (SHARIE B., AGE 12)

"I don't have any idea, and even if I did, I would have no comment." (RILEY, AGE 9)

"Maybe it's a symbol for something, like the patriots and the British . . . and the Dolphins." (laughs)
(ROB, AGE 11)

"Nice animals . . . but you have to keep them in their cages." (LUCILLE, AGE 6)

20. "First Lady"

"The first girlfriend a guy ever has."
(JOHN, AGE 9)

"She's like a queen, but we don't have any here in America." (JERRY, AGE 10)

"Same as the first man, except you hear more about it." (MICHAEL, AGE 10)

"It could be anybody. . . . If there was a girl who swam the Mississippi River, and no girl had done the whole thing before, then she would be the First Lady." (VINCENT, AGE 9)

"A person who looks nice in Bill Blass evening wear." (MARCI, AGE 13)

"It's silly. . . . Why should women be given a role like that? . . . Women should be President and Vice President, and idiots like Dan Quayle should be doing something safe, like being a salesman."

(CARLY, AGE 13)

"The first lady was Eve." (MARVIN, AGE 10)

"It's Barbara Bush now, but Nancy Reagan still thinks that she is the First Lady!"

(CELESTE, AGE 11)

"My mother is the first one in her family."

(ROXANNE, AGE 6)

"Mrs. Bush, and her dog is the first dog!"

(JIMMY U., AGE 9)

21. "Camp David"

"Where the Boy Scouts meet."

(JEREMY L., AGE 8)

"A fun place where kids go when their dad has two weeks off of work." (MARVIN, AGE 10)

"Where the government is in Israel."

(ILENE, AGE 9)

"It's the main place David Letterman spends his summers." (CHARLENE, AGE 10)

"There's counselors and servants there."

(MORTON, AGE 7)

"Maybe where the army does its shooting for practice and where they have to run around the tanks."

(SCOTT, AGE 12)

"Camp David is the place the President goes to think when there is too much noise in the capital."
(RITA, AGE 11)

"It's from the Bible. . . . It's where that King David knocked off the giant." (CHRIS P., AGE 8)

"Camp David? I don't know. . . . We haven't had a President named David, I don't think. . . . Are you sure it's not something else? . . . Maybe it's Camp Ronald." (KIT, AGE 11)

22. "The Hot Line"

"It's the name of the President's hot tub!"
(MANDY P., AGE 11)

"It's the President's private phone. . . . He probably calls long distance too much." (WENDY, AGE 11)

"It's the number you call for the hospital."
(RUDY, AGE 9)

"Something in Texas that divides where the United States is and where Mexico is . . . They call it the 'hot line' because they eat all those hot tacos and ancholados down there." (REID, AGE 10)

"The number is 1-900-9009, and you are supposed to ask for Tony!" (TONY, AGE 12)

"A place where teenagers can call and talk to each other about sex . . . It costs a lot, though."
(ANN, AGE 10)

"The telephone between the Soviets and the Americans . . . It's like a fax machine, except they use it more. They even ask what they want for dinner when they visit each other." (JAY, AGE 10)

"The state line between Washington, D.C., and the rest of the country." (PAM, AGE 11)

"Maybe it's something in the President's kitchen?"
(PAULA F., AGE 8)

"The hot line is a secret thing, so I'm not supposed to say." (BERNIE, AGE 7)

23. "Speaker of the House"

"My mother . . . She does all the talking in the family." (ALVIN, AGE 9)

"It's the guy who tells you the President is coming and he tells the TV people to shut up so everybody else can hear." (BARBARA, AGE 10)

"It means a big radio that you have on the shelf all the time." (JOHN, AGE 9)

"The person who owns the Capitol and all the others have to pay rent to." (IVORY, AGE 10)

"The big sound system they have when the President gives a speech outdoors . . . That way all the people can hear him real good." (KIMBERLY, AGE 10)

"Used to be Jim Wright. I don't know who it is now. They change them all the time."
(HARVEY, AGE 13)

"The person who is the leader in the Senate . . . He tells the others to shut up, except if he likes what they have to say." (DUSTIN, AGE 12)

"The guy who got fired for cheating on his taxes." (PATRICE, AGE 11)

"The one with the big hammer who gets your attention when the President is ready to answer some questions." (GINGER, AGE 12)

"A man who the President picks . . . They usually eat a lot." (TODD T., AGE 8)

"A Speaker of the House is someone in the White House whose job is to run up and down the halls and give them messages real quick." (OLIVE, AGE 8)

24. "Super Tuesday"

"A fun day for the whole family."
(ROGER, AGE 10)

"It's when 'The Wonder Years' is on."
(MALA, AGE 7)

"It's a recognized hollow-day." (OLIVIA, AGE 8)

"It has to do with Superman and the *Daily Planet.* . . . But he's fake and the President is real."
(ALVIN, AGE 9)

"Super Tuesday? When the President meets with Gorbacoff?" (BERT Y., AGE 13)

"The day after Super Monday!"

(TERRY, AGE 12)

"A big football game at the Capitol."

(MARVIN, AGE 10)

"I don't know that one. . . . Ask me about how they elect somebody for President."

(GEORGE J., AGE 9)

"What people like my dad say when it's a Tuesday and the weather is nice . . . 'How's it going, Jim?' . . . 'Great; isn't it a super Tuesday?' . . . Something like that." (EARL, AGE 10)

"It sounds real dumb, but I don't know what it is."

(ANGELA, AGE 8)

"Super Tuesday is when the Democrats and the Republicans play a softball game and try hard to beat each other. . . . They have fights a lot, so they have to stop the game early. Some get real mad because they don't get another turn at hitting."

(FRANK, AGE 9)

"I think it's an election before they get to run for President. I guess they have it on a Tuesday, but I don't know what's so super about it."

(DONALD, AGE 12)

"I'll pass on that one." (ROSE, AGE 7)

"Super Tuesday is Election Day, when everyone goes to vote for a person they want or the lesser of two evils. . . . That's what my dad says."

(SEAN, AGE 10)

"Must be a new holiday. Maybe we'll get it off from school." (MARCIA W., AGE 11)

"Super Tuesday is the Tuesday after Christmas and right before the New Year's Eve. It's when nobody is really working and they're all taking it easy and wishing the rest of the year was like this."

(TRISHA, AGE 11)

★ *4* ★

"The Bushes Don't Care if Their Grandchildren Don't Flush the Toilet!"

Children Provide the "Inside Scoop" on Life in the White House

*T*elevision and the news media provide us with some revealing images of the Presidents and their families. Journalists like Sam Donaldson and Barbara Walters are quick to respond to our fascination with the private affairs of our leading citizens. Influenced by these images, and contributing a natural thirst for gossip in their own right, youngsters are eager to try to describe what goes on behind the closed doors of the White House. They have their own unadulterated ideas about what the President does for fun, about what he says to the Vice President or the First Lady in private conversations, and just about any activity that a President might engage in.

There are limits to what the professional journalists can tell us about the President. Unshackled by such journalistic restraint and such mundane details as obtaining access to the President, kids are free to *tell all* in great detail and living color. Their boundless imaginations furnish a wealth of juicy personal material. No presidential act or decision, however unofficial and off the record, is considered taboo!

As you explore the world of the children's imagination, you may sense that the children see the President in a definite way. They are motivated to make the President more *human*—and to reduce the perceived distance between the President and the rest of the country. These youngsters imagine the President and his family and friends involved in all kinds of mundane yet familiar activities—the President is seen going to Disneyland; the First Lady is pictured as an avid cardplayer; or the Vice President is depicted wagering on professional football!

In these images the world of Washington is brought home to the child. Often through the use of humor, youngsters are able to picture a place that otherwise might seem formal and foreign to them. Such joking about the Presidents is wholly consistent with the American tradition. Youngsters have little affection for distant monarchs or figureheads, but instead prefer to envision real people in important positions who have the same needs and foibles as the rest of us. The presidential figures created by the children may speak for the American people, but they do not stand above them.

1. On What Most People Don't Know About the President

"He has sex every night of the year!"

(SELINA, AGE 13)

"He eats Toosie Roll Pops!"   (SHEILA, AGE 8)

"George Bush is really a member of Hari Krishnas."

(BARRY, AGE 12)

"He used to be a fire-eater in the circus."

(REID, AGE 10)

"The President is really a Democrat."

(MARCI, AGE 13)

"He didn't shave till he was thirty. . . . And then he only shaves with an electric razor."

(ALPHONSO, AGE 13)

"Maybe President Bush smokes cigars, but he doesn't like people to see it. He might get criticized for giving people a way to get cancer."

(SANDY, AGE 12)

"I heard he always wanted to be a baseball player. But maybe he is happy now, since he does not have

to play in the minor leagues in places like Paw-
tucket." (LEE R., AGE 9)

"The President wears Snoopy pajamas when he goes
to bed." (MARIE, AGE 7)

"The President might cry a lot about world problems
when he is alone." (ROBIN, AGE 12)

"Today, people know everything about the President. That's what TV is for!"
(CAMILLE, AGE 13)

"He is really a quiet Protestant guy who doesn't like
a lot of attention." (AL, AGE 10)

"The President didn't eat all of his vegetables when
he was a kid, and that's why he's skinny now."
(PAUL, AGE 11)

"President Bush is a liberal dresser when he goes out
on the town." (MARVIN, AGE 10)

"He might not like parts of the country like California or South Dakota, but he's got to act like he does
because he is President of every state. . . . Plus he
won't get elected again if he was not fair."
(BARRY, AGE 9)

"He watches 'Jake and the Fatman.'"
(JOE G., AGE 10)

"I bet he doesn't like to go for a haircut on account
of he is losing his hair already!"
(RANDY, AGE 13)

"Bush probably reads a lot. Books and newspapers and magazines. Like *USA Today*... He doesn't have much time, so he has to get the ones with pictures all over the place. . . . His assistants fill him in on the rest." (SIMON F., AGE 10)

"He was once a used-car dealer!"
(DOUG F., AGE 9)

"The President is my kind of man. I think he's cute, but don't tell his wife or she might get jealous!"
(MELISSA SUE, AGE 6)

2. On What the President and the Vice President Talk about Privately

"Gardening." (TINA, AGE 12)

"They talk about hobbies like bowling."
(LAURIE, AGE 13)

"They talk about where the best Italian restaurants are." (BRYN, AGE 9)

"They talk about the weather all the time, like my dad does with the people he works with."
(JIM, AGE 9)

"They talk about that lady Kim Basinger."
(BARRY, AGE 12)

"Bush probably talks about what Quayle should say at his next speech. . . . And then Quayle probably

says: 'Yes, sir, I was thinking about that myself.' "
(GORDIE, AGE 11)

"They figure out strategies on the Russians and the
Germans." (MYRON, AGE 9)

"Bush and Quayle don't say much to each other at
all. Bush figures out ways to keep Quayle from talking too much and not giving out secrets to the Democrats." (JENNIFER, AGE 12)

"They trade recipes." (WANDA, AGE 12)

"The same as everybody else . . . They talk about
which teams are better, like the Redskins and the
Forty-niners." (SEAN, AGE 10)

"They ask each other: 'How's your family? How's
your dog?' " (PERRY, AGE 7)

"Mostly nothing. They stand around and spit."
(SAM, AGE 8)

"They figure out what places to give money to and
what places will be poor." (ALVIN, AGE 9)

"They make sure they got their stories straight."
(RILEY, AGE 11)

"What would happen if President Bush got sick or
hurt—they have to be prepared so people don't
have to go out and vote again."
(ROBERTA, AGE 13)

"Girls!"   (BOOMER, AGE 8)

"How they got everyone fooled thinking they were working hard."   (CAMILLE, AGE 10)

"What they are going to do with Phil Donalson!"
(I.E., SAM DONALDSON; AS RELATED BY
ANDREA, AGE 10)

"They talk about which movies are good and which are dirty."   (ROGER, AGE 11)

"They gossip about the Treasury and the generals in the army."   (ALBERT, AGE 13)

"How they don't get along."   (JILL, AGE 11)

"The President and the Vice President talk a lot. To relax and take it easy, they talk about football. I bet they bet on big games like my dad does."
(HARRY, AGE 12)

3. On Whom the President Consults with, When He Is Trying to Decide If the Country Should Go to War

"The President checks with his mother—to see if it is okay with her. Then, if she gives the go-ahead, then so does he."   (KENT, AGE 8)

"He calls those pilots who fly those B-50's."
(BOB M., AGE 13)

"President George Bush might talk to his wife, Barbara. But he talks to other people too, because she is probably so nice that she is always against war."
(CHANDRA, AGE 9)

"He checks with the Vice President and with the Israelis." (VANCE, AGE 9)

"He talks with the television men at CNN."
(CARL, AGE 10)

"He makes chitty-chat with Billy Graham."
(TAMARA, AGE 13)

"Maybe he talks it over with Dan Quayle. But maybe not." (RUSSELL, AGE 10)

"He phones up that Schwarzie guy in Saudia Arabia." (BRET, AGE 12)

"Maybe he listens to the senators that agree with him." (MARIE H., AGE 9)

"He sends a letter to Ronald Reagan, and Ronald Reagan writes him back when he gets a chance."
(MICHAEL M., AGE 11)

"He asks for the opinions of the army generals and the navy people too. If there is a tie, he is in a fix. So he might have the Coast Guard vote to break the tie." (JASON G., AGE 10)

4. On the President's Least Favorite Person
(Living or Deceased)

"He might not like the Pope because the President is not Catholic, I don't think." (BRAD, AGE 10)

"That's easy. Saddam Hussein. That guy is like the Godfather. Except he is real."
(DAVID S., AGE 11)

"Maybe he hates Bill Laimbeer of the Pistons, like my father does." (BRET, AGE 12)

"Hussein. Because he took over Kuwait and he hurt a lot of people. Bush said he was like Hitler, and that Hitler wasn't real popular either."
(BARBARA Y., AGE 9)

"He probably can't stand the person who thought up broccoli." (CARL, AGE 10)

"He might not like Dana Carvey, because he tries to imitate him." (GEORGE E., AGE 11)

"Maybe he doesn't like some of the reporters who criticize him. If you don't have something good to say, you shouldn't say nothing."
(JASON G., AGE 10)

"He probably doesn't like it when all the tourists try to steal his socks as a souvenir."
(MONICA, AGE 12)

"If he knows about him, he wouldn't like Billy Idol too much." (CHANDRA, AGE 9)

5. Concerning How the President Gets Ready Before a Big Speech

"President Bush wears extra cologne because many people go up and shake his hand afterward."

(CELESTE, AGE 11)

"Before a big speech about money, the President looks in the mirror and talks to himself. He might be superstitious, so he might look in his wallet and carry a rabbit's foot there." (SANDRA, AGE 12)

"He usually makes sure he gets the food out of his teeth with dental floss." (RONNIE, AGE 13)

"He puts his wig on!" (SEAN, AGE 10)

"He gargles with Listerine, and his wife listens to him so many times, she gets a headache.... Then he practices on his advisers to be sure. . . . They get bored, too, but they don't have a choice. It's their job." (COURTNEY, AGE 9)

"If the President was a woman, she would spend a lot of time doing her makeup and making sure her dress and shoes matched." (CYBIL, AGE 10)

"He shoots breath spray in his mouth and sings: 'ME, ME, ME!' " (GERRY, AGE 7)

"I think President Bush doesn't practice that much. He just tries to be himself and gives his speech just like he wrote it. He tries to be honest with the people and tries to forget about all the cameras and lights and the millions of people. . . . But President Reagan was different." (HERB, AGE 13)

"I don't think he memorizes the speeches, because he can see the words on the television he looks into. . . . He just sleeps before the speech."
(CHARLIE, AGE 11)

"I don't think Bush eats much for dinner before the speech because it might make him have . . . well, it might make him feel funny when he's up there. You know, he might get stomach problems like you get after you eat like Mexican food."
(CHRIS, AGE 9)

"He might go for a walk in the city and check out the action." (MARVIN, AGE 10)

"He yells at his speech writers until they write what he wants!" (QUENTIN, AGE 13)

"He checks his spelling because he is no good at it. . . . Neither am I . . . Maybe I could be President someday!" (JOANNIE, AGE 8)

6. About What the President Does When He's Mad at Congress

"He swears like a maniac!" (CHARLIE, AGE 10)

"He could throw an expensive vase across the room." (CAMILLE, AGE 13)

"He tells them he won't have them over for lunch no more unless they start playing the game his way." (GORDIE, AGE 11)

"The President stands on a chair and stomps his feet." (LAUREN, AGE 12)

"He reminds 'em that things could be a lot worse. . . . Dan Quayle could be President!" (BARRY, AGE 12)

"The President has to go to the bathroom!" (JOHN, AGE 8)

"He gets red and has a deep breath and he holds on to it for ten seconds." (ELISSA, AGE 10)

"Tries to get gossip on the Congress . . . Like he tries to find out which ones are cross-dressers." (MARCI, AGE 13)

"The President turns red but not too red or someone will think he's a Communist!" (ALVIN, AGE 10)

"They all meet at the Capitol at midnight and they check the Constitution to see who is right." (CORY, AGE 11)

"He goes to his psychologist, who tells him it all has to do with his childhood." (KENDRA, AGE 12)

"The President stands by the flag and then he calms down." (MARIA, AGE 8)

"The President writes them a nasty letter and tells them exactly what he thinks of them. They have to edit out the bad words like 'idiots.' "
(CONNIE, AGE 9)

"He makes all the senators go back to Congress school and learn what he wants them to."
(BOBBI, AGE 8)

7. About What Foreign Leaders Most Often Ask About When They Visit the President

"They ask why there isn't a woman President yet."
(CHER, AGE 10)

"Nobody knows. . . . It's a secret. But probably they talk about trading guns." (JIM, AGE 9)

"They say: 'Hey, how come if this is a democracy, you're living so high on the hog?' "
(ANITA, AGE 12)

"Foreigners ask about how he won being President."
(WENDY, AGE 9)

"They might want to see the country. So they ask for the President to take them to the Statue of Liberty and then to Disneyland . . . so when they get back, they can tell their people that they went there."

(MYRON, AGE 11)

"They want to know: 'Where's the beach?'"

(EILEEN, AGE 10)

"They talk about swapping wives."

(TENLEY, AGE 12)

"They want to know what's for breakfast and where you can get good Chinese food!"

(LEIGH, AGE 11)

"The visitors may want to know if President Bush is happy." (NORM, AGE 8)

"It depends where they're from. The Japanese may want to know about cars, but the English may want to have some tea." (MINDY, AGE 12)

"They might talk about basketball players from the Europe countries who want to come here and how they would do in the NBA."

(CARLOS, AGE 11)

"They say: 'What's the cover charge at some of your swinging night places?'" (WALTER, AGE 10)

"Hey, Georgie . . . where do you hide your vodka around here?" (GORDIE, AGE 11)

8. Concerning the President's Secret Communications

"He sends most of his messages by carrier pigeon."
(JASMINE, AGE 11)

"He puts an ad in the yellow pages."
(HARVEY, AGE 10)

"The President can hire a plane that does skywriting in Russia!"   (PHIL, AGE 9)

"Everybody can't know about all that's going on, that's obvious. That's why the President has the Secret Service. They keep everything to themselves or they'll be called traitors. They would get in plenty of trouble."   (NANCY, AGE 11)

"He has to tell the Vice President what is going on. They might even have a secret language that only they can understand."   (TONY, AGE 11)

"The President has a red phone he uses to call Russia, but he can't use it a lot because the long distance costs too much."   (SARI, AGE 10)

"I've wondered how they keep secrets. But I don't see how they could. . . . Somebody will blab!"
(GLORIA, AGE 9)

"He has to make sure all the information about the army and tanks is in secret computers, so the Russians and the China leaders won't know what we have in store for them."   (BRYN, AGE 13)

"The President shouldn't keep any secrets.... That's not nice." (FRAN, AGE 6)

"He has to have a secret place to keep all the information about all the spaceships that land on the earth.... They keep it all a big secret because they think people would be scared of things that look like E.T." (STANLEY K., AGE 8)

9. About the President and the First Lady's Spare Time

"The Bushes like to be with kids. That's why they have all the grandkids over and they don't even care if they make a big mess in the White House living room or they don't flush the toilets!"
(FRANK, AGE 9)

"About every two weeks they go on a fox hunt!"
(BRYN, AGE 13)

"They count their wrinkles." (TONI, AGE 12)

"They go to the movies and kiss."
(JERROLD, AGE 10)

"They get on a stage and talk about drugs till they're blue in the face ... pretty much all day."
(AMANDA, AGE 12)

"Cooking. The President might be able to do a few of his favorites, like New Orleans food or something he used to eat in Texas, which maybe his wife don't know how to dish up." (CYNTHIA, AGE 12)

"They are very busy and have no free time. They have to serve the people, otherwise they will have to find other jobs where they have to work in an office and don't get a free house." (JIMMY, AGE 9)

"The favorite thing they like to do is just spend time in their mansion." (MARCI, AGE 13)

"They might go to a workout club. She might do aerobics and he does the Nautilus."
(BETTY, AGE 12)

"They play kickball!" (BENJI, AGE 7)

"I don't know. . . . Maybe they play golf, like my parents do. The Bushes don't seem like they could hit the ball too far, but they might like to relax. . . . Maybe they only play three holes and then drink cold drinks like maragitos!"
(SANDY, AGE 12)

"She probably sews and he watches himself on television and they talk about the people they like and the ones they don't like." (ERIC, AGE 9)

"They call their families on the hot line."
(JEROME, AGE 8)

"They play chess when there are no people looking."
(RYAN, AGE 9)

"They visit sick kids in hospitals."
(CHARLES, AGE 9)

"They go to Disneyland and zoos and places that adults have vacations. They probably wear sunglasses all the time so people know they're famous."
(LISA, AGE 10)

"They scare kids to death about drugs."
(KYLE, AGE 11)

"They visit their friends in Russia."
(CLINT, AGE 9)

"They meet their relatives and try to remember their names." (JAN, AGE 10)

"They like to eat jelly beans. They eat hundreds. They get them free." [HOW?] "Ronald Reagan got his jelly beans from Japan to keep the peace."
(SAMANTHA, AGE 12)

"When they have no work to do, they probably smooch like teenagers!" (giggle)
(GLORIA K., AGE 7)

"They eat oatmeal cookies and drink milk and sit by a fireplace and plan for when they retire."
(BLAKE R., AGE 10)

10. What Most People Don't Know about Living in the White House

"There's no dogs allowed there since they might ruin the bushes and trees." (RYAN J., AGE 13)

"They serve steak and macaroni for breakfast there!" (CLARK, AGE 9)

"They got plenty of mice there."

(ALBERT, AGE 10)

"It's a nice place to visit, but I wouldn't want to work there." (ANITA, AGE 12)

"They have to do their own cleaning."

(ANDREA, AGE 10)

"They don't allow pets. I'm not sure about kids."

(KYLE, AGE 11)

"The beds aren't made! Ever!" (RANDY, AGE 13)

"They have eighty-three televisions so they can watch all the news stations and see what they are saying about them." (BART, AGE 8)

"There are ghosts there. From the early days of the U.S. And they still keep an eye on today's events." [CAN YOU NAME ONE?] "I think his name is Carter." (SHEILA, AGE 10)

"It's really pretty boring. They miss being close to the people and going shopping and going to the beach." (LAURA, AGE 8)

"Every room is a different color. Some are even polka-dotted!" (SETA, AGE 10)

"There are some pictures of ladies without clothes on mixed in with the ones of the Presidents!"

(FELIX, AGE 9)

"It's not really a good place to live, 'cause you're always afraid you might break something—like an old lamp or an old statue of a President."
(BRYAN, AGE 10)

"They don't have much private space. It's strange."
(KATIE, AGE 10)

"The White House is not the first one. The other one burned down. I hope they have a good fire department there now." (NOLAN, AGE 12)

"It's old-fashioned. They have oil lamps and they even could write with feathers."
(CARLETON, AGE 13)

"I've been there. Most people think it's in the sticks, but it's right there in the city. You just have to wait in a line for a long time." (BOB, AGE 10)

"Nobody knows for sure exactly what goes on there, and the people who do know will never tell you."
(GLORIA, AGE 7)

11. About the Evening Conversations of the President and the President's Family

"They talk about the thousand points of light. . . . That's the reason they stay up so late."
(TERI, AGE 12)

"The Bushes don't talk. . . . They just read each other's lips!" (GORDIE, AGE 11)

"They say to each other: 'We did a good job with the country today. We deserve a treat. Do we have any ice cream in the refrigerator? Let's make some milk shakes in that blender we got from the Reagans.' "
(SHEILA, AGE 8)

"They watch TV and don't talk to each other."
(PAUL, AGE 11)

"They talk about war and things that bother them."
(BARRY, AGE 9)

"They talk about moving to Kuwait!"
(MARCI, AGE 13)

"Mostly they talk about problems, like crime and drugs. . . . Boy, they must have trouble sleeping at night." (ELISSA, AGE 10)

"I bet they have sherry and talk about all the money they have." (CAROL, AGE 9)

"President Bush and Barbara Bush may talk over what the President did that day, and she listens good and tells him what he did wrong."
(STEPH, AGE 10)

"They talk about gossip, like how Wade Boggs had a sex affair." (CARMINE, AGE 11)

"They like to have guests over for dinner, and get free of government talk and talk about other things, like movies and books and other people, and tell silly jokes and play charades."
(JEANNE, AGE 12)

"They sneak away to a motel to relax and to let go of their hairs!" (BUD, AGE 9)

"The Bushes start to plan what they will do in Maine. They try to make the weekend last for three days even when it's no holiday."

(MARK Z., AGE 13)

"They decide who to invite over and who to be cold to because they don't like them, because those people criticized the President or talked behind his back about politics." (CHERYL, AGE 11)

12. The President's Favorite Television Shows

"He watches 'Sesame Street' because he is a fan of Bert and Ernie!" (J.R., AGE 9)

"He likes *Revenge of the Nerds II* for obvious reasons." (JOHN, AGE 8)

"'Looney Tunes'—it reminds him of Washington!"

(OLIVIA, AGE 9)

"Reagan used to like *Rambo,* but Bush probably watches old 'Father Knows Best' reruns."

(JIMMY, AGE 9)

"Barbara and President Bush like to watch Dr. Ruth for sex tips." (ROBERTA, AGE 12)

"They watch 'Who's the Boss?' and the President always yells: 'I am!'" (HANK J., AGE 11)

"The President watches 'The Cosby Show' and 'A Different World' so people won't think he has prejudice." (MARVIN, AGE 10)

"In the morning, he likes to get up and do his exercises with Richard Simmons."
(MARCI, AGE 13)

"Mr. and Mrs. Bush watch 'America's Home Videos.' . . . They like to see all of the voters acting silly. Then they know they got nothing to worry about."
(BARRY, AGE 12)

"He [the President] never watches the news. . . . He can't stand Dan Rather!" (RICHIE, AGE 11)

13. On Some Typical Things That the President Says While He Is Watching the News

"Yea . . . That's my army . . . Way to go, boys!"
(RUSSELL, AGE 10)

"I hate looking at Hussein. Get his picture off the screen." (DAN, AGE 8)

"Can I take my gas mask off now?"
(BEV K., AGE 12)

"That guy who reads the news is a real stiff."
(MICHAEL M., AGE 11)

"Every time I watch the news I can't digest my dinner." (AFTON, AGE 12)

"Hey, I just remembered. We're missing 'Growing Pains'!" (JASON G., AGE 10)

"Gee, I'm a pretty good-looking guy."
(CHANDRA, AGE 9)

"Those dummies don't know what they're talking about. . . . If they only knew the truth."
(VANCE, AGE 9)

"You know, Barbara, I wish I didn't have to send those soldiers to Saudi Arabia . . . It makes me sad."
(BARBARA Y., AGE 9)

"How come they don't have the weather on this channel? I want to go fishing tomorrow."
(MARIE H., AGE 9)

14. About the President's Office

"There's a secret door there that leads to a tunnel that goes all the way to the Capitol, so the President can sneak in and talk to people there."
(RYAN, AGE 9)

"My friend Jerry says the President has a whole stack of *Playboy*s there!" (GEORGE, AGE 10)

"It's big . . . real big. . . . He's got a big desk with a picture of Barbara Bush there. And he's got plenty of files and papers there. Everything is push-button. All he has to do is push one button, and the defense people and the assistants all come in like they're doing a fifty-yard dash!"

(DENNY, AGE 13)

"It's right there next to his bed. That way he can work at night, and even call other countries if he can't sleep." (GAEL, AGE 8)

"I think the office might be where the Congress is. The President gets up early and he goes out and has eggs and toast. Then they drive him to his office until he gets tired. That's about twelve o'clock. Then he goes home for the day." (DAVE, AGE 8)

"He might have one of those golf sets in his office . . . a plastic putter and a green to practice on. . . . But he would have to put all that in the closet when the foreign people come to talk."

(JERRY, AGE 10)

"It's where he does his homework. But I bet he's got plenty of food there to keep him going . . . and a lot of Coke, too." (LISA, AGE 7)

"He has a couch there to take naps on, or to sleep on when he works late and doesn't want to wake Mrs. Bush with his snoring." (SALLY, AGE 9)

"His place is decorated in gold and he has a secret crown he puts on when nobody is looking and he is all by himself!" (SUSIE, AGE 8)

15. Concerning the President's Plane

"There's always a bartender on board!"
(CHERYL, AGE 13)

"It can fly faster than regular planes, but you never hear anything about it." (JEROME, AGE 10)

"It's red, white, and blue all over."
(RENEE, AGE 8)

"They probably have plenty of movies on there for all the flights to Europe." (ROBIN, AGE 12)

"It has to be pretty big so all the fat reporters can travel with him!" (TERRY, AGE 13)

"I think it's called *Air Force One*. I don't know if it's the same one President Reagan had. . . . President Bush's plane is probably smaller."
(CARL, AGE 11)

"It has toilet paper with Mike Dukakis on it, left over from the election." (MARCI, AGE 13)

"I didn't know he owned one. Is he rich?"
(JILL, AGE 7)

"It might be like the ones America Airlines has. It has girls who walk up and down the aisles and act real friendly and give you free food and milk. It might have a guy whose voice you hear on the loud-speaker, and there's a pilot, too. . . . I wonder if they have to wear seat belts, too. . . . I hope they can't crash like the regular airlines."

(CHARLIE, AGE 10)

"I know that the President used to be a pilot, so maybe he flies it himself sometimes. Does Dan Quayle know how to fly?" (GERARD, AGE 10)

"He's got more room for his legs than other people do." (KATARINA, AGE 8)

16. Some of the President's Favorite Sayings

"Shut up and sit down, Dan!" (GWEN, AGE 13)

"Better dead than a Democrat!"

(STEVEN K., AGE 10)

"You're a liberal, Barbara!" (CAROL, AGE 12)

"Be kind and gentle." (ROBERTA, AGE 12)

"Well, I'll be a monkey's uncle!"

(SEAN, AGE 10)

"Break a leg, Dan." (MARVIN, AGE 10)

"Where's the zoo here?" (JOHN, AGE 8)

"By gosh, what do I do now?" (JIM, AGE 9)

"What the hell, I'll do it my way."

(CLETE, AGE 11)

"Read my lips. . . . I'll punch you out!"
(RICK, AGE 9)

"Servants! Servants!" (MARY T., AGE 8)

"I can't believe it myself. . . . I'm the President!"
(TOM R., AGE 11)

"Don't worry, be happy with your taxes."
(EUGENE, AGE 13)

"He might like to go to baseball games and yell: 'Kill the umpire!'" (LEON B., AGE 12)

"God bless America and the democracy we are trying hard to get." (MARY JANE, AGE 8)

"Barbara, tomorrow is the next day of the rest of the time we have in this great big house."
(LAMARR, AGE 13)

17. Thoughts on the President's Favorite States

"He likes Alaska the best because it's not on the mainland and they don't give him any trouble."
(SHERRY, AGE 11)

"California, since all the California girls are there!"
(ROBIN, AGE 12)

"It's Connecticut. . . . It makes President Bush feel better that Governor O'Neill is going bald, too!"
(MADELEINE, AGE 13)

"Mental anguish is the state he is always in because of all his problems." (MARCI, AGE 13)

"I know for one hundred percent sure it ain't Massachusetts!" (HENRY, AGE 11)

"He doesn't like to pick favorites. They are all the same to him. Even Idaho!" (JON, AGE 10)

"Must be Maine.... He spends more time there than anywhere else." (HELENE, AGE 9)

"Nevada is his favorite. . . . Want to know why? . . . Because prostitution is legal there!"
(ROBIN, AGE 12)

"I would say Texas since that is the last place he moved to." (CAROL, AGE 12)

"Washington . . . Why else would he live there?"
(LIZZIE, AGE 8)

"He would love Georgia. Everyone does. We got a beautiful state, but we got lousy sports teams, though. Still, it's nice." (GINA, AGE 12)

"Florida . . . There's a lot to do there, and they voted for him, too." (SALLY ANN, AGE 8)

"State? Hmm . . . Maybe one of the Dakotas." [WHY ONE OF THE DAKOTAS?] "Because he might want to be on that mountain with the big Presidents."
(MIKE P., AGE 10)

18. On the Marital Relations of the President and the First Lady

"I figure they don't have much time for marriage stuff, since they only have a few hours to sleep."
(ELISSA, AGE 10)

"They might get along like my parents do. . . . Everything is okay up there." (BOB, AGE 10)

"They love each other and they love those Bush kids and little kids, too. . . . My mother says they should call them 'shrubs.'" (BETTY D., AGE 9)

"I am sure that Barbara Bush would be easy to get along with. You never know; *he* might be, too."
(SANDY, AGE 12)

"President Bush is probably a real romantic type when he is alone and not in front of the crowds."
(FRANK, AGE 9)

"It must be hard. They can't take walks off the White House land or anything. . . . Just because they are old doesn't mean they aren't like other married people."
(SHERRY, AGE 11)

"I wonder if her hair bothers him because everybody jokes about it." (SHEILA, AGE 11)

"My mother says that they are kinda cold to each other. . . . I'll have to look more to see."
(TRUDI, AGE 10)

"They should kiss all the time."
(MEREDITH G., AGE 6)

"Their relationship is real good. . . . He tells her all about the government, even the top secret information, so she doesn't feel left out and she has something to talk to her friends about."
(KIM, AGE 9)

19. On How Things Would Be Different if the President Were a Woman

"Nothing would be changed . . . except everybody would say: 'Yes, ma'am' instead of 'Yes, sir'!"
(CLIFTON, AGE 11)

"The world would be a better place!"
(KENDRA, AGE 12)

"The President would have to wear two earrings instead of one!"   (TERRY, AGE 13)

"The President would walk different."
(ELISSA, AGE 10)

"There would be more romance in the White House, especially if she wasn't married."
(HEATHER K., AGE 9)

"The food would be better there."
(ANGELICA, AGE 8)

"He'd have to change his name to Georgette!"
(MARVIN, AGE 10)

"All the other countries would have better manners when they deal with the U.S."

(ANITA, AGE 12)

"All the bodyguards would have to be girls, too."

(ROB O., AGE 12)

"Her husband would be in a weird position. Would he stop working? It would be interesting."

(VALERIE L., AGE 12)

"If they made a statue of her in Washington, it sure wouldn't be a naked one!" (CORY, AGE 11)

20. Concerning What the President Will Do after He Leaves Office

"He'll co-host a talk show with Gorbachev, and they'll try to beat everybody else in the ratings."

(BARRY, AGE 12)

"Start his own Georgie Bush Fan Club!"

(ALICIA, AGE 11)

"He will have a President's library in Maine, and there will be a lot of books about him there."

(GORDIE, AGE 11)

"He might sing country-western songs."

(CHERYL, AGE 13)

"He'll go fishing and try to forget all those years as President." (ALLAN Y., AGE 12)

"Give speeches and go to a bunch of dinners where they will toast him and name streets and cities after him." (MITCH, AGE 8)

"Maybe he will be an adviser to President Quayle." (GLORIA, AGE 9)

"If I were him, I'd go to all the amusement parks in the country. . . . They might let him in free!" (ARTHUR M., AGE 8)

"He'll make a lot of money. . . . You can count on it!" (MARVIN, AGE 10)

"Write a book about all that happened and make sure that some publisher pays him good for it." (TERI, AGE 12)

"He should try to change the laws and run again. . . . Keep on going!" (RALPH P., AGE 11)

"He and Barbara Bush will go stay with the Reagans." (FRANK, AGE 9)

"He will keep in touch with all his friends all over the world, and he could have a few in Washington, too." (BARBARA F., AGE 11)

"Bush will costar in a movie with Ronald Reagan" (LARRY V., AGE 10)

"He'll have a good, long laugh about what just happened for the last eight years." (GERRY L., AGE 11)

21. About How the President and the First Lady Would Like to Be Remembered by the American People

"For their great doctor, Dr. Sid Klotzman."
(STEPHANIE, AGE 12)

"How they fought drugs and won the war."
(KARL, AGE 11)

"They'd want people to say they were real nice and kind and didn't steal anything from people."
(MARLON, AGE 7)

"They'd want people to leave them alone so they can get some peace and quiet!"
(SHAWNA, AGE 9)

"The people should remember them in their prayers and not hate them if they have to raise taxes. . . . They [the Bushes] didn't mean to do it. It just happened by accident." (REID, AGE 10)

"We should remember them as more kind and gentle than most of the Presidents." (STEPH, AGE 10)

"Just as good Bush people." (AURELIO, AGE 7)

"They would like to feel like they added to the country and left a good mark on the White House—kept it good for the next boarders."
(PETER L., AGE 9)

"They would like us to say: 'Thanks for the memories, George and Barbara.' " (BART J., AGE 11)

"The Bushes would like America to see that they helped us and brought more peace to the world and got better relations with the Middle East and Russia. And they wouldn't want any big thanks afterward . . . just a few handshakes and kisses."

(MARTI, AGE 12)

Chop! Chop!

Gino (age 13)

* 5 *

Once Upon a White House
Children's Stories about the Presidents

*E*veryone loves a good story, and children are no exception. Once youngsters have selected a main character (otherwise known as an innocent former President), they will weave an intriguing plot in no time. Masters of political detail, children will enthusiastically create a cliff-hanger, a happy ending, or even a romantic vignette. Even political scandals are not beyond their repertoire.

When it comes to the Presidents, children's stories are strikingly informative, telling you just how they see life in Washington. Some of the boys sound like former Speaker "Tip" O'Neill, as he speaks about his years on Capitol Hill and his relationships with the various Presidents. The girls resemble women Cabinet members, former First Ladies, or even Justice Sandra Day O'Connor, as they reflect on life in the nation's forefront. In their efforts to present true-to-life images of our leaders, past and present, each child helps us to appreciate the Presidents in highly realistic and human terms. Mindful of their responsibility to history and to future generations, youngsters relate their colorful narratives with some dedication to accuracy along with a penchant for generous embellishment.

Children ordinarily tell stories about famous and familiar Presidents, but not always. "Who are these strange men who appear on our paper money and coins?" the kids wonder. "Why aren't there any women?" some youngsters may ponder. These and many other subtle questions underlie the children's vignettes.

Youngsters use their stories to grow closer to the Presidents or to create a morality play about American life. The children really do appear to be curious about American history, but theirs is a curiosity that dry textbooks alone will not satisfy. They want to get to know the Presidents and picture them as real people, not just as historical figures.

Throughout all the stories, the youngsters demonstrate a considerable interest in what a President is concerned about. What mattered most to Abe Lincoln, Theodore Roosevelt, or even Ronald Reagan? Was it the country, or was it fame and their own continued presence in the White House? Most of the older children recognize that the Presidents may have some self-interest at stake, though nearly all the youngsters also appreciate a President's loyalty to America.

The stories also offer a child's view of American history. The children have a quiet method behind their make-believe stories. Amid the stories of attention-seeking Presidents and those who have been forgotten by many of us, there emerges a relentless search for the truth. The children want to know what these Presidents were like and what the roles they assumed in shaping the destiny of our country.

★ ★ ★

Stories about George Washington

"This is about our first President, General George Washington, who is famous no matter how you look at it. He was the father of our country. He was just a farmer, but one day that all changed. The British massacred the whole city of Boston, so we had to stand up and fight. George took command and told the British guys where to go (I think it was Philadelphia).

"In the end, he got his own city named after him, but he had to step down since he wasn't a king or an emperor or a Russian. I am not sure how long it took for this, or what he did after that. Maybe he took a tour and made speeches. But his birthday is always a big deal (everybody gets it off from school), and like I said, he is famous for sure.

"Oh yeah, I think maybe he had something to do with the Constitution, but I might be wrong. Also there are now sports teams with his name, like the Washington Redskins, but he doesn't know about it since it happened in the twentieth century. After he was dead."

(AS TOLD BY KEITH, AGE 9)

"One day George Washington went into the house and called his friends over. And when they came over, they had a party. He only did that because his wife, Nancy, went out to eat with her friends and he wanted to go with them, but she said no! So he decided to have a party himself. When his wife caught him red-handed, he said his friends snuck in here. So he had to kick the friends out.

"Then there is another story about a cherry tree, but that one shows another view of him."

(RELATED BY EVELYN, AGE 10)

"George Washington was home real late at night. He was playing Nintendo for a while. Then he drank lots of coffee. Then his wife came in and they played hide-and-go-seek.

"They were happy then. You know it."

(BY MELANIE, AGE 9)

"Washington was the great man of our country. Maybe the greatest. He fought the Indians and he made sure they didn't give us any trouble. He fought the British soldiers and gave them a lickin', too. He was real good at these wars, and that's how we got good at war, too."

(AS OFFERED BY BLAKE, AGE 9)

"George Washington went to school one day. But he didn't sleep good last night and so he was not very awake. When the teacher called on him to state all the Presidents, he could not think of any yet. So he said that he wanted to be President someday.

"The rest is history."

(AS NOTED BY TROY, AGE 8)

"On a big, sunny day, Washington the President got elected. There was no one else running, but he was afraid he might get surprised. He was sure glad the campaigns were over. So he had a big party with flags and made a big speech. They even decided to have a big ball (the same as like today). People had to pay a lot to dress up and go, and that is how they started having coins and money in the Treasury."

(BY MEGAN, AGE 7)

"My story is about George Washington. He was a cool dude who took out the British and paved the way so that there was freedom and no taxes. Enough said."

(VOLUNTEERED BY MARVIN, AGE 10)

"Once there was a man named George who listened to his mother and father. They told him not to lie and he didn't. Not ever. He told the truth at church, at school, and at home, too.

"Then once he was walking in the woods and he

came across a mean bear. The bear said to him: 'Hey, George, where are you going? You better not be going across the Delaware waters.'

"George didn't know what to say 'cause that was where he was going. He was goin' to cut across the Delaware. But if he told the truth, the bear might eat him up. What should he do?

"He had to think quick. He had some food in his pocket, so he gave it to the bear. But the bear said, 'That was only peanut butter, and I like honey.'

"Then George said, 'My name is Washington and I am going to be famous someday.' But the bear did not believe him and the bear was getting meaner.

"So finally George had to make something up. He told the bear that he was going to a place named Washington and they had lots of honey stored away there. He didn't say anything at all about the Delaware.

"The bear believed him and he figured, besides, George might turn out famous and then he could brag that he almost ate him."

(BY MARCUS, AGE 11)

★ ★ ★

A Tale of Two Adamses

"There was a father and a son. Two Adamses. The father was a President and he said to the son, 'You will be a President, too.'

"But then the son said, 'No, Father, I want to be a millionaire.'

"And the father said, 'It's the same thing.'

"So the son became a President, too. His name was Quincy and he was rich for many years."

(AS RECOUNTED BY JILL, AGE 8)

"He followed George Washington as President. His name was John. I don't know if he is part of the Adams family in Massachusetts, which is where I live. Do you?

"I don't mean to be stupid, but I don't think he is known for much. It is hard when you are second. I know, 'cause I have an older brother and two older sisters.

"Maybe John fought about the War for Independence. Against the Redcoats. That's England.

"He must have owned a muskrat and he probably knew Paul Revere, at least enough to say hello to and say: 'Nice shot.' "

(BY RANDALL, AGE 10)

★ ★ ★

Stories about That Fine Statesman, Thomas Jefferson

"Thomas Jefferson was one of the early and first heroes of our country. He was from Virginia and he wrote the Declaration of Independence. Maybe he got some help with the printing.

"But he owned slaves, too, which not all the American people know. Nobody is perfect, but in those days they didn't totally know right from wrong. He was good on the writing, but he didn't always practice what he preached.

"I don't know for certain how he got to be President, but his writing may have made him real popular, and that was all he needed to get out the vote.

"Today there's a memorial building for him and he is considered almost like Lincoln. Except Lincoln freed the slaves, and that makes him better."

(EXPLAINED BY SELINA, AGE 11)

"Once upon a White House time there were friends named George Washington and Tom Jefferson. They were like Huck Finn and Tom Sawyer. They did everything together. Fight for freedom and stuff like hunting, too.

"Tom was younger, and so he was nice to old George. But he was jealous, too. He wanted to be first, and old George got the job. He was the President. It pays to be honest, and George was not a liar. Tom was not either, but like I said, he was younger.

"Even if you are honest, you still have to wait if you are younger. Tom got his chance later on and he made it stick."

(BY PAUL, AGE 10)

"Thomas Jefferson was the smartest President we ever had. He probably had an IQ of over two hundred!

"If you look at all the others, all forty, they might not be anywhere close to that.

"But they got other good things going for them. They have good personalities!"

(By BARCLAY, AGE 12)

★ ★ ★
A Story about James Madison

"Once there was a President named James Madison. He had a school that was named after him because he was one of the early, early Presidents. It's a big brick school. It's real old. And it doesn't have much of a playground at all. It's easy to hit a ball into the street there.

"The teachers there are real old, too.

"It's not much fun to go to school there.

"I know 'cause I got friends there.

"James Madison would be upset if he saw it."

(By JUAN, AGE 12)

★ ★ ★
A Tale of Andrew Jackson

"He's pretty well-known. I've heard of him. But I don't know much about him. Still, I wanted to do something besides Washington and Lincoln. So if it's okay, I'll make up a story.

"Andy Jackson grew up as a red-white-and-blue loyal American. He must have lived around 1800 or 1810 and so was probably pretty excited that it was a new century. Like kids today who are curious about what 2000 will be like. Anyways, Andy was a regular kid except that he was extra patriotic. He always wanted to grow up to be President.

When the big day came, he was so happy, he cried. But his wife told him not to cry. She said that people would think he was a wimp if they saw him. So he put away his hankie and started to give his first speech as President. But he got all choked up and had to stop. His wife told him to try again, and sure enough, he couldn't do it.

"So she gave it for him. When it came to the Bible oath part, he did it himself. Otherwise it wouldn't count and we would have one less of the forty-one Presidents.

"But thanks to his wife, Andy is on the list."

(BY CLAIRE, AGE 10)

★ ★ ★

The Many Yarns about Abraham Lincoln

"Abraham Lincoln was elected President in 1861 and he had a topped hat and a suit. He stopped being the President in 1865.

"In all those years he was President, he was real funny. But to be President now, you have to be good on TV. Not in those years, when they didn't have it.

But now you do. That's how people find out if you got the talent. Like Abraham Lincoln had."

(BY CARL, AGE 10)

"Lincoln was the best President. He knew just what to say to the people, and he cared a lot about everybody. He was shot for his beliefs. We should all not forgot him and remember that he was a great President.

"Even if we moved his birthday to not right on the day he was born."

(BY GIGI, AGE 8)

"Lincoln grew up in a log cabin that was small and old. He might have ate maple syrup and pancakes like they serve at the International House of Pancakes. But probably not much else. He was poor.

"That's why in pictures he looks skinny and almost ugly. He didn't eat much. Plus he was busy being President."

(BY WARREN T., AGE 10)

"President Lincoln was a great man who stood up for what he believed in. He was against how uppity the South was and how they had slaves, and so he told them: "You Dixies, you better mind your manners and salute the flag of the United States, not the South flag. Or else we are going to come down to your plantations and farms and take away your slaves and bring them to the North to be part of our economy here."

(BY JEREMY B., AGE 11)

"His name was Abe Lincoln and he was one of the most famous Presidents. He lived many years ago, but his speeches are still read today. People are still trying to figure out what he said since it is so hard and complicated. That's why we study it in school.

"But older people should read it, too. They might learn something."

(BY J.P., AGE 9)

"After the Civil War was over, Abraham Lincoln put his feet up and relaxed for a while.

"But he never got the chance to enjoy the peace. A killer came in and shot him.

"Even though the war was over, it was not all better. There was still a lot of hatred. But at least the slaves were free and we did not lose any states.

"If we had lost states, there might be no Florida or anything. It was a close call."

(BY CAROLINE, AGE 9)

★ ★ ★

A Story about Andrew Johnson
(Or Is It Lyndon?)

"Andrew Johnson was the President when we fought the Vietnam people. He made some mistakes, so everybody told him to quit and let someone else take over. I think he may have been the Vice President when the President was shot, but I'm not sure.

"One thing I don't understand is why he is on a list of Presidents after Lincoln, when he should be with

152
★

all the ones who are modern. Maybe it's just out of order."

(BY CHARLIE, AGE 11)

★ ★ ★

Some Tidbits about Ulysses Grant

"He was a general for the North in the Civil War, which is also called the war between the fifty states. He helped the North win by having good tactics. Outside of this, he was President after Abraham Lincoln, but mostly he must have taken it easy since no one was ready for more change. Also he felt he was entitled to a rest because he had worked so hard to protect the Union and smear the other side.

"As far as private stuff goes, I bet he smoked a lot of big cigars while he was President. I've seen pictures, and he looks like the type who would."

(BY KIRBY, AGE 12)

"There is a tomb where he is buried, not like a regular grave. It has all kinds of evil spirits around it. Witches and vampires and weird ghosts who look like they lived in Washington hundreds of years ago.

"Nobody knows for sure about this, but it could be. I don't know if you can visit the tomb. It probably is too weird.

"I wouldn't want to go. I'd have to be forced to go in. And if I did, I'd bring some protection. I'd bring a cross with me!"

(BY RAFAEL, AGE 8)

★ ★ ★

The Truth about Rutherford B. Hayes, the Forgotten President

"My story is about Rutherford B. Hayes. I picked him because I knew nobody else would. It is not nice to be left out. Also, this way I could be original. He needs a person to stand up for him.

"Rutherford was a poor boy, I'm not sure from where, who grew up to be President after the Civil War. He must have helped the nation get it back together. But who knows much about him? He has not got any respect. Probably the people back then made fun of him because his name was Rutherford. People shouldn't do that. His mother named him, so it wasn't his fault. Besides, it is wrong. Grover Clevelands is not a name to write home about either.

"I think we should have a Rutherford Hayes Society. We should write our congressman and make sure he is better-known! He should be taught more in history classes. And we should put him on a big money amount. Like a hundred-thousand-dollar bill!

"I volunteer to be President of this volunteer society. The only thing I ask for is that I would get the first hundred-thousand-dollar bill.

"That would be justice for everybody after all."

(AS PASSIONATELY TOLD BY WAYNE, AGE 12)

★ ★ ★

Equal Time for Grover Cleveland

"Many years ago a man grew up in Ohio and was very, very eager to be famous. He wanted to be real bad. So he figured he would run for President of the United States someday. He was ready to try real hard and not quit no matter what happened.

"First he was a senator, and that was good. The voters could see who he was. But that was not enough. He waited many, many years. And he was getting tired.

"Finally he got his chance and he became the President. He was so excited, he decided to make a new city. He wanted the city to be the capital. But we already had one, and since the White House was there and they couldn't move it, the capital would have to stay put.

"To make him feel better, they named the other city after him. It's still Cleveland today."

(AN ORIGINAL STORY BY RISA, AGE 10)

★ ★ ★

A Quick Salute to Theodore Roosevelt

"Theodore R. was playing tag one night and he was playing fierce. But he tripped over a rock and hurt his knee. No blood, just hurt.

"Franklin Roosevelt helped him up.

"That's what relations are for.

"The end."

(MANUEL, AGE 10)

"His nickname was 'Teddy,' but he was no teddy bear. He fought in a lot of wars and was the President.

"A President cannot be a teddy bear. That's obvious."

(LISA P., AGE 9)

★ ★ ★

The Legacy of Franklin Roosevelt

"Franklin Roosevelt is my choice because he was our leader during a challenging time. He was President when Pearl Harbor was bombed. But he stood up and said: 'This day will live in infamy; let's go get the Japanese and bomb them!'

"It's not that he liked violence. He had no choice, because we were attacked in Hawaii. Even though that is not right nearby, it is part of our country.

"Plus it's stupid that they bombed Hawaii since it's supposed to be such a nice place. In those days, the Japanese must have been crazy!"

(FROM THE ACCOUNT OF LARRY, AGE 11)

"Franklin was a skinny kid with glasses, and all the kids used to make fun of him. Why? Because he had a funny name like Franklin.

" 'Franklin, you're a loser,' they would say. 'Franklin, you may be rich, but you're still dumb!'

"He showed them, though. He grew up and became their President. He proved that even if you are not a popular kid, you can be a popular guy in the government when you grow up.

"Of course, all the girls in the United States started liking him then, too."

(BO'S STORY, AGE 9)

★ ★ ★

A Few Facts about Harry Truman

"He was a man who was President after the World War. I think he must have been glad he was President when he was, or he would have to fight the Nazis from Germany. And that jerk Hitler.

"Still, it was not easy for Truman. He probably had to fight Communists and gangsters here at home. Here in the U.S. When he left, people still liked him.

"Oh, one more thing I remembered. I think when he won the President, he was supposed to lose. But he just squeaked by and surprised the whole country.

"It must have been exciting when you had no idea who was going to win."

(SANDY V., AGE 12)

★ ★ ★

Stories about John F. Kennedy

"There was a President about thirty years old who was President when my mom and dad were kids. He liked every person, and every person liked him. He was young and they thought he would be cool to have as President, and maybe for many years.

"But he was killed just like that. Nobody knows who did it or why. But people were sad for many years, and some may even be today.

"He had brothers in the government, too, but the only one left is a senator named Ted.

"I don't think Kennedy was as big as Washington or maybe Reagan might be someday, but you never know. He could have been a big President, too, if he had the chance."

(As passed along by Ray, age 11)

"One summer John Kennedy and all his brothers were out near the ocean playing. There was Bob and all the others, too. They were a close family and joking a lot. They played football and volleyball, too.

"Then they started having an argument. It was over something small, like who would play and who would keep score. Everyone wanted to play. The girls [the sisters] wanted to play, too.

"Then the parents came out and yelled at them. They told them that they were ashamed at how they were fightin'. And then they said, 'Look how bad it would look if people knew you were fighting. If you want to grow up and be Presidents and senators and officials, you can't act like this. You have to act better. The next time you act like this, we won't take you to the beach. Is that understood?'

"John and his brothers and sisters nodded. They didn't like getting yelled at, but they didn't want to get hit, which would be the next step if their father had his way.

"Another thing was that they wanted to be a success and grow up and be tops in the country. They figured their parents might be right.

"So they learned to get along pretty well. They stopped yelling and complaining. Or else they made sure their parents never found out about it."

(SHARED BY CARIE, AGE 13)

★ ★ ★

The Hard-to-Explain Presidency of Gerald Ford

"A few years ago, Gerald Ford was President. He was a nice man and most of the American people liked him. He seemed like one of us and was very straight with the questions he was asked. There was peace then, too, and it stayed peace while he was President. No one argued much.

"But he was not elected again. I don't know why.

"What did he do as the President?"

(BY THE INQUISITIVE MOLLIE, AGE 10)

"Gerald Ford made the Ford car, and it's the best-seller in the world.

"I know about that because my mother has a Ford and she likes it very much, and my father has one and he says it's very comfortable for an American car.

"When I grow up, I'm going to get one of those cars, too. The ones that Gerald Ford started."

(BY THE CAR ENTHUSIAST, STEVEN, AGE 9)

★ ★ ★

Anecdotes about James "Jimmy" Carter

"Jimmy Carter was watching TV and he saw Ronald Reagan on so he changed the channel. Then he saw 'Alf' was on, and he thought that was stupid, too. So he switched to cable, but he didn't have the good channels, and there was only reruns.

"So he went out and drove to the video store and looked for a video movie he liked. They didn't have *E.T.*, but he found some crime movies and some other family stuff. Then he was happy and he said, 'Boy, I'm sure glad. I never got to do this when I was President.'

"So he got home and put the family stuff on and he figured that maybe it was good he was only President for a little while. It's good to have some freedom, too."

(BY MARLENE, AGE 12)

"Carter was from Georgia and he liked peanuts a whole lot. Even more than ice cream and popcorn. But he was kinda sloppy with the peanuts and they are still cleaning up after him in the White House. They still find some in parts of his office.

"A President should be neater and clean up his place."

(BY THE IMMACULATE SHANNON, AGE 11)

★ ★ ★

A Few Screenplays about Ronald Reagan, Never Before Seen in His Movies

"After he retired, Ronald Reagan didn't know what to do. He was bored, so he started calling all the girls he knew. Most of them said they were busy. Some didn't like him 'cause they were Democrats.

"But then he called Vanna White, and she said, 'Come on over. I will be your friend as soon as I finish the "Wheel of Fortune" today.'

"Ronald Reagan was glad, but he didn't want anyone to know about it or it would be in all the headline newspapers. So he just gets together with her in secret hideaways likes caves and tree houses."

(BY TYLER, AGE 11)

"One day I saw President Ronald Reagan go to the store. I ran and asked him for some money. He said that he could give me three dollars. And he gave it to me. I went to the store and I bought some flowers for my mom.

"She asked me, 'Where did you get the money from?'

"I said I got it from one of the Presidents.

"She said, 'What President?'

"I said, 'Reagan.'

"So then I got punished."

(BY YVETTE, AGE 10)

"Once upon a time it was early in the morning and the President was thinking about people in Africa. He was feeling sorry for them. He had heard it on the news that they were not getting enough food. So President Reagan went to work at the big dome in Washington. When he was finished with being President of the United States for that day, then he was tired, but he said he'd try to raise a little money for Africa."

(BY JENNY, AGE 8)

"President Reagan was a bad actor. I saw that *Bedtime for Bonzo,* and it was *Boring Time for Bonzo!*

"I don't think Presidents should do other things like acting or sports or television. They should have their mind on the country and how to make peace all over the world."

(BY THE OPINIONATED SUE, AGE 11)

★ ★ ★

Up-to-Date Stories about George Bush

"He is a big baseball fan. One day George was watching the Mets versus the Cubs and they scored a ton of runs. The Mets scored forty-five and the Cubs scored forty-four. It was a long game. George was happy when the game was over.

"Then he could go back to running the country, but he had to see who won first."

(AS RECORDED BY SPORTS REPORTER PAUL, AGE 10)

"George Bush is about President number forty. We've had a lot, but he's the most important because he's in there right now.

"Give him a few years. Then we'll see if he stays important."

(BY ANITA, AGE 11)

"Georgie got in his red car and drove real fast down the highway. Ninety miles an hour! The police followed him and stopped him to give him a ticket. When they saw who it was, they didn't know what to do. So they told him to have his limo-seen driver do the driving from now on."

(AS UNCOVERED BY DAN T., AGE 9)

"President Bush was having a bad day. There were problems all over the world. There were too many drugs in the city, and he was getting disliked by the people.

"So Bush came up with an idea. He decided to give away free TVs to folks all over the world. So he took the money and he sent TVs all over the place. Mostly colored TVs with VCRs! To China and to Russia, too.

"Everybody was real happy. They figured if he could do that, maybe he could stop drugs, too."

(BY CORLISS, AGE 10)

"Bush and Reagan went horseback riding one afternoon, and Reagan said to Bush: 'I'm sure glad you took over after me. That Dukakis guy was a jerk!'

"And Bush said to Reagan, 'Yeah, that would have made two in a row!'"

(BY TERI, AGE 12)

"It was a winter day and there was nothing to do. So President George Bush decided to go out and get a haircut. He found a place with a red, white, and blue pole and walked in. The barber said, 'What can I do for you, sir?'

"President Bush said, 'Just give me a shave and a regular haircut, please.'

"So they started on the haircut and got to talking. The barber told President Bush all about his family, and President Bush talked all about politics.

"When it was over, President Bush invited the barber to the White House and told him to bring his grandkids.

"The barber was excited and he wouldn't let President Bush pay for the haircut.

"Since then, President Bush goes out a lot and

visits people like doctors and dentists and grocery store people. And the same thing happens. He figures that if this keeps up, he might never have to pay for anything again."

(BY DAVE, AGE 11)

Shannon (age 11)

★ *6* ★

"Dear Mr. President, Do You Really Get to Meet the Super Bowl Champs?"

Children's Letters to the President

*P*rovided with the opportunity to write to the President of the United States, or other powerful figures, what do boys and girls choose to say? What specific topics, political or everyday concerns, do youngsters address in their correspondence with our chief executive?

Children are concerned about the state of international affairs and the position of America in the world. They are also opinionated about life here at home—even if they may be a bit foggy about some domestic issues. Among the most common political subjects children write about are the following: international relations, nuclear war, space exploration, the President's power, race relations, the drug problem, crime, the environment, and domestic affairs.

Youngsters don't hesitate about sharing a personal concern with the President now and then, and it is these letters that are often among the most memorable. Some kids see the President as a potential adviser and confidant, while others are just plain curious. They want to know what's going on in the White House! A bold youngster may even offer a little unsolicited advice to the President. The range of personal subjects defies an adult's imagination, but a partial summary would include such topics as: the child's personal ambitions, family affairs, friendships and loyalties, career interests, confusions and worries, and that perennial concern of children—kids' rights and fairness.

Letters are an intriguing way for children to express their deepest feelings and creative ideas. When it comes to their letters to the President, the correspondence may turn into artful satire. Sometimes inadvertently, sometimes purposefully, the children help us to laugh at ourselves and at our leaders, too. Their words are never frivolous but often are a means of revealing their underlying view of our nation—about what our priorities are and what the kids think they should be. We can read the letters for their humor and playfulness, but also bear in mind the thought-provoking messages that some are being conveyed.

★ ★ ★
The Letters

Dear Mr. Bush,

If you run for President again, make sure you got Nikes on your feet. They are better for them.
I hope that you run fast enough to win.

>Love,
>José (AGE 9)

★

Dear Mr. President,

Help South Africa. Nelson Mandela is cute. You should like him too.

>Valerie (AGE 9)

★

Dear Mr. President,

What do you eat for lunch when you entertain fancy people from other lands?
I bet you eat crowsonts and cabbiar and foreign stuff like that.

>Bye,
>Wayne (AGE 10)

★

Dear Mr. Reagan:

I was sad to hear that you had to leave the office of being President. What will you do now?
If you get bored you could come visit me here. My

parents never voted for you at all, but they still might let you come in the house.

Michelle (AGE 8)

★

Dear Mr. President,

I want to be the first kid in space. I weigh 110 pounds so I would not take up much weightless space. So send me up there. You won't be sorry.

Woody (AGE 10)

★

Dear President Bush,

My uncle says I talk like a politician. What does that mean? I thought maybe you would know since you are one.

Love,
John F. (AGE 9)

★

Dear President Bush,

When do you think there will be a black President? I think there should be one soon otherwise that would mean there is a lot of prejudice. Plus it would be good for getting along with other countries who may get messed up by the change. They might give in to what we want.

Robert (AGE 9)

★

Dear President,

My dream is to meet you some day. Honest. I would love to visit you in the Capital. Do you know how you always have the World Series Champs and the Super Bowl winners over right after?

Maybe we could meet on one of those times so I could say hello to them too.

> Your friend,
> Roger (AGE 11)

★

Dear Prez,

I have an idea about all the $$$ we owe. Why don't we sell some of the schools and teachers that are government's property?

> Anonymous
> (male, AGE 9)

★

Dear President George Bush,

It is good that we talk to Russia more now. But please don't trust them altogether. They could hide a few bombs and we would not know about it. Maybe in some place like Alaska. Or they might have some spies right here in America.

> Love,
> Camille (AGE 10)

★

Dear Mr. President,

Please do more for the homeless. You and me would not like to sleep outside and ask for money either. It is a real problem and it is not they're fault at all. I even gave my lunch money to help. I know you will try hard. Please.

Thank you,
Stephanie (AGE 8)

★

Dear President Bush,

Bring our people home safe and don't let the Iraq leaders blow up the airports here. We need them to take trips.

Jason G. (AGE 10)

★

Dear Mr. President,

You are doing a good job with being the President. I wouldn't like to think all the time like you do. Mostly about war.

Sincerely,
Celeste (AGE 9)

★

Dear Mr. President,

I hope you are safe. None of those missiles can make it all the way over here. Can they?

Barbara Y. (AGE 9)

★

Dear President,

This war may hurt our economy. Plan ahead more next time.

Manuel (AGE 12)

★

Dear Mr. George Bush.

I am glad that you said this fighting is not like Vietnam. That war was bad and we lost a lot of good men there.

Good luck to you. I am praying for you and for our troops and our friends that are fighting with us.

Do you think you will get elected again?

> Best of luck
> Myron (AGE 11)

★

Dear Mr. President:

What I want to know is this. Why don't you paint the White House another color? Some color with more color in it.

Like maybe black and silver. That would look awesome.

> Hi,
> Reid (AGE 10)

★

To the President,

What did you really think of the last election? Pretty mean, I thought. My dad says you like it that way. The same as people like to watch wrestlers.

> Sean (AGE 10)

★

Dear Mister President,

I want to wish you good luck in running our country. I will also think of you in my prayers. I will pray that you do not have to deal with any big problems like a war. Because who knows for sure if you could handle them.

> Goodbye,
> Dwight (AGE 10)

★

President,

> No more stupid pet tricks with your dog, please!
> Kirsten (AGE 8)

★

Dear Mr. Bush,

> Do you like girls with white hair better?
> Luv,
> Angelica (AGE 8)

★

For the President,

> I want to know if you lived in Shakespeare's time, what character would you be?
> There's a brain-twister for you,
> Quentin (AGE 13)

★

Dear President,

> Do you talk to ordinary people a lot on the telephone or are you too busy? Ever talk to kids?
> Lots of love and kisses,
> Serena (AGE 8)

★

Dear Bush.

I don't care much for republicans but I'll give you one chance.

Curtis S. (AGE 11)

To George Bush,

I want to congratulate you on being President and wish you luck. Especially I want to say good luck on fighting drugs and alcohol abuse. You see people high on the street or at games all the time.

Maybe you could make liquor a crime just like the drugs. Try it and see what happens.

Sincerely,

Jesse (AGE 11)

Dear President,

We need to plant more flowers and trees. Right there where you live there's too much cement. We should take away some of the cement and make everything more green instead of gray!

Tonya (AGE 7)

Dear President Bush and V.P. Quayle:

Too many people have no homes and too many people have hunger. It is very sad. Please help them. You should be the main ones to say people should give money to help. Maybe you could have a special show where people give pledges?

You might not be as big as the show on Labor Day

right when school starts, the one Jerry Lewis is on, but every little bit helps.

Cory S. (AGE 9)

★

Dear Mr. President,

How many vacations do you take a year? My father says you take too many. He only gets one.

Byron (AGE 10)

★

President Bush:

Be tough on terrorists! They're like the evil we learn about in Church.

Brooke (AGE 9)

★

Dear Mr. President Bush,

How do you decide what to wear in the morning? How come most of your ties are all red and blue? Don't you have any white ones?

A friendly fan,
Danny W. (AGE 9)

★

Dear Barbara Bush,

I think you are a fine lady and a good first one too. I wonder how you like your job and also what exactly you do?

Your friend,
Vincent (AGE 9)

★

Dear Mister Bush, the President.

What does it take to be a President? Do you need to be real smart or just lucky?

Do you need to have a lot of money to run for President or just a lot of friends?

I would appreciate an answer.

> Thank you,
> Herschel (AGE 9)

★

To Ronald Reagan
In care of the White House

I hope this letter gets to you. I saw you in the broadcast booth at the all-star game on TV. You seemed like you were shy. How come? Was it because you were out of touch with baseball?

I hope you aren't feeling too old. The U.S. may still need you.

> Keith C. (AGE 10)

★

President Bush

I would like to ask you if you liked school when you were 7. I like it pretty much besides the subjects we have to learn.

> Best wishes,
> Gerry (AGE 7)

★

Dear President bush,

This is Tyronne Kemp. I'm ten years-old and I'm in the fifth grade. I want to say some things I think you should do as the President.

I want you to collect all the weapons in our state so we don't have to be bothered any more. People are killing the animals such as elephants and alligators. Also the animals with fur.

Please help them and help us too.

Sincerely yours,
Tyronne Kemp (AGE 10)

Mr. Bush,

Don't just give the people on the streets money and food. Give them your love and your heart.

Amanda (AGE 8)

Dear President Bush.

You are a nice President but you could be nicer if you made the taxes lower. How about it?

By,
Ian (AGE 9)

To George Bush:

I heard you went to Yale. I live in Connecticut so I know about Yale. When you went there was it still in Connecticut? Or somewhere else—like in England.

Phyllis (AGE 9)

Dear Mr. President,

How do you pick the people who work under you. Do they have to be Republicans or just plain Americans?

> Your sincerely friend,
> Angie (AGE 9)

★

Dear Mr. President,

I have a poem for you. It goes like this.

I hope you have a nice day.
I hope you do your work in a nice way.
And then can take it easy by the bay.
> Signed,
> Miguel (AGE 10)

★

To the President,

I wish I was the president so I could live in that house. I would have big dinner partys just like you.
> Gretchen (AGE 8)

★

Dear Mr. and Mrs. Bush.

I would like it if you made a new law. ALLOW DOGS AND CATS INTO ALL BUILDINGS.
Snakes might be too much to ask for.
> Sam (AGE 9)

★

Dear Abraham Lincoln,

I would like to see you in the White House. When will you be there?

Just kidding!

Matina (AGE 7)

★

Dear President George,

Here are some tips on how to make our country better. Like cleaning the litter. And people should be less to vote. But they should still be over ten.

Also give people jobs instead of them having to be qualified.

Sincerely,
Leon (AGE 9)

★

Dear Mister President:

My parents say that if you had them pay more taxes they wouldn't vote for you again.

You should listen. That's two votes and you might need them.

Plus we have plenty of aunts and uncles and cousins too!

Josh B. (AGE 10)

★

Dear Mr. Bush,

I think you are doing a good job. I hope your drug plan works, since I will soon be a teenager myself.

Thank you,
Cynthia S. (AGE 12)

★

★————————————————————————————————★

Dear President of the United States,

I wonder if you will get my letter or it will go to a secretary who says thanks and signs your name for you.

Jan M. (AGE 13)

★

Dear George.

I wish you could cut all the taxes to a penny.

Love,
Steph (AGE 10)

★

Dear Mr. Bush,

Could you help me? Could you tell all the girls at school to get along so they could do cheerleads for the games? Thank you.

Love,
Rolanda (AGE 10)

★

Dear President,

I don't want you to get sick because if you got sick you could not give rules to people. Then Mr. Kwhale would be there but he might not know all the rules.

by Rick (AGE 8)

★

To the President of America,

You are just like a father to us. Really, I mean it.

Alphonse (AGE 11)

★

President Bush,

I want to know if you are going to take people off welfare because I got friends on welfare. I didn't want them to move because they are the only friends I got. So please don't take people off welfare. I hope you don't.

> Sincerely yours,
> Corinne (AGE 11)

★

Dear President,

How are you? I was voting for you all the way, and tell Barbara Bush I said hi.

George, you should put the price of taxes lower. I want some Mattell stuff that is too much money right now.

> Keith (AGE 10)

★

Dear Mr. President,

Do your best for the *people* and the *people* will do their best for you.

> Best wishes,
> Roger T. (AGE 12)

★

Dear President George Bush—

I am Robert Thomas.

I think you should support nuclear power to avoid the changing prices in foreign oil. You should support legislators raises so they won't need other jobs and miss meetings. Please turn down the repealing

wage law. Contractors don't need $200,000 per year!
Don't leave Quayle in charge of drugs. He won't run
it effectively.

Congratulations on being President and good luck.
>Sincerely,
>Robert Thomas (AGE 12)

Dear Mrs. Bush,

Help the homeless and those peoples who can't
read. And keep bugging Mr. Bush so he doesn't forget!
>Didi (AGE 9)

Dear Mr. President,

>What do you like to do?
>Personally, I like swimming and canoes.
>That's my taste.
>What's yours?
>>Don K. (AGE 9)

Dear President George Bush,

>What do you think of Gorbachoff?
>Do you think he's just a big show off?
>>Perry (AGE 11)

★

Dear President Number 41,

You must be real proud to be a President! Think
about all you can do. You can even send a rocket to
the moon or even another planet!

But you should get rid of drugs the first thing. It's a bad mark on the country.

Marcie (AGE 10)

★

To the White House,

I love you, Georgie.

Elaine J. (AGE 6)

★

Dear Vice-President Quayle,

How's it going? Do you like being the Vice President or were you happier in the Senate? Do you miss Indiana?

I am from New Hampshire and I would miss it if I had to move. It would take something real important.

That's why I wanted to know what you thought of living there.

Best luck,
Kevin L. (AGE 11)

★

Dear President Bush,

I am going to give you a report card just like we get. Here is your report card so far.

speeches—C+
leading the country—B
friendly—A−
kind and gentle—incomplete

Rhondi (AGE 11)

★

Dear Mister President.

Why is school so long? By the time it's over (3 o'clock), half the day is gone!

John F. (AGE 8)

★

Dear Mr. President,
Twinkle, twinkle little star
How I wonder what the White House looks like.
Up above the city so high
Is it like a place I know?

Pamela (AGE 9)

★

Dear George,

Your speeches are boring. You need a better writer and some jokes. You should ask Arsenio Hall for help.
You would get peoples' attention more that way.

Spencer (AGE 13)

★

Dear Mister President,

You are just like my grandfather, Walter Fredickson, Sr. He is kind and gentle and he likes to take it easy and sleep.

Goodbye,
Sarah F. (AGE 9)

★

For the President,

The best way to get the hostages out is to bomb Lebanon. True, this might hurt some people, but let's face it, nothing is easy in this world.

Nicholas L. (AGE 12)

★

Dear President,

We need more ethics all the way around. Make the teachers teach it!

Anonymous (AGE 8)

★

To the First Lady,

Women should have more rights and equal pay. I think you should get the same salary your husband gets. Don't you agree?

I hope this doesn't cause you any marriage problems.

Lana (AGE 11)

★

Dear Sir,

What video games do you play in your spare time? I bet you have a lot of fun. You must play games like russian rulette!

Best wishes,
Steven (AGE 9)

★

Dear Mr. President.

Keep America out of war, please. If we have one in the next ten or fifteen years, I might have to fight in it. And I get sick on planes and boats.

Deron B. (AGE 10)

★

Dear Mr. Bush,

I am glad you came into our schools on the TV to talk about drugs. But why don't you drop in more often to show you really care?

It would help you get votes in my community too.

Love,
Cindy (AGE 8)

★

Dear Mr. President,

I like you for many reasons. One of them is because you are left-handed. So am I.

People like us are destined for being stars.

Your friend,
Anthony C. (AGE 9)

★

Dear Mr. President,

What do you think about all those changes in Poland? I think it's good if they get rid of the Communist dictators and the Church takes over instead. It's better if they are the ones telling people what to do.

Sue Marie (AGE 11)

★

Dear Mr. President,

I admire you because you worked so hard to get where you are and didn't have to cheat much along the way!

Jason T. (AGE 9)

★

Letter for George Bush

Why do you always say the thing about reading your lips. Why don't you just say what you mean? You shouldn't play games with the citizens. We aren't deaf!

Evelyn (AGE 10)

★

Dear President,

You are very popular at my school. So is the Flag. We are very patriotic and try hard to be good. We always have a lot of special ceremonies at American holidays like President's Day and St. Patrick's Day.

Maybe sometime you could come for one. Halloween is a good one 'cause it's really fun and you could dress up as a vampire and no one would no who you are!

Holden (AGE 7)

★

Dear Mr. President,

Who do you look up to? Who is your hero? I would like to know.

It's okay if it's a football player. I won't think it's silly.

Mine is probably Dan Marino, but I like Bernie Kosar too.

But I wouldn't mind being a rich owner of one of the teams either.

> Hi,
> Vince R. (AGE 10)

Dear George:

You finally made it to the top! I am glad for you. I know you were trying for all those years.

> Lori (AGE 9)

Dear Mr. President,

What did you think of the Teenage Mutant Ninja Turtles movie? I thought it was good.

What would you do if one of the turtles came out of the sewers in Washington, D.C., and said—Cowabunga, George!

> Your friend,
> Ellis (AGE 9)

Dear President Bush,

Are you a good father? You better be. 'Cause you got a whole country to support!

> Duane (AGE 10)

★

To the First Lady,

My mother likes you a lot. She says you are down in the earth.

Love,
Carol Ann (AGE 10)

★

Hey Mr. President Bush,

Why don't you stop by here on your way up to Maine next time? All you have to do is get off the turnpike and drive about a mile. We have a white house, same as you.

It would be fun,
Joanne (AGE 8)

★

Dear President,

I seen you exercising a lot on the news. I like to get a lot of exercise too. But I'm glad there isn't no gang of cameras following me around, because I got some fat on me.

But I'm trying hard to get rid of it. Just like you.

Ryan (AGE 9)

★

Dear President,

We learned at school that there are so many changes happening in the world that they are going to have to write the history books over.

I feel you should keep the changes going if they are good changes. We can have something else besides history for a little while. Like maybe extra gym.

> Sincerely,
> Joe (AGE 11)

To the White House,

What do you do there for fun on the Fourth of July? Do you have any good fireworks?

I bet you have the kind that stay up for ever. Like maybe four years!

> Charlie (AGE 12)

★

Dear President of the United States,

When your mail comes, does the mailman put it all in one mailbox? It must be plenty big. I bet you must get a lot of fun letters, but you must get a lot of bills too since it is such a big country.

You could always keep your old mail in the Washington Monument. There's room there and it's not too far from your house.

> Sincerely and truly yours,
> Raymond (AGE 9)

Mary Jane (age 9)

★ 7 ★

Conclusion

What Political Messages Are the Children Conveying?

It is extremely challenging to sift through hundreds of lengthy interviews and discern what our children may be collectively telling us. Since the individuality of the children stands out so much, generalizations are hard to come by, and even more difficult to be certain about. Yet in the course of being with the children and reviewing their answers again and again, I did begin to notice trends among the youngsters that transcend their backgrounds and individual personality differences. These subtle trends are truly one means of communicating children's thoughts about the political realm to the adult world.

As you read through the chapters, you probably formed your own impressions of what stands out in the comments of these youngsters. I would encourage you to think some more about what the children are saying, but here are my intuitions based on the interviews.

(1) THE CHILDREN WANT THE PRESIDENT TO BE ACCESSIBLE. In comment after comment, and particularly in many of their letters, the kids attempt to approach the President in friendly and amicable ways. Many kids want to enter into a dialogue with the President or have direct contact. Yet at the same time, they see Washington as a pretty faraway place.

The youngsters would like to be privy to the President's plans for the country and his views on contemporary matters, particularly President Bush, who is currently holding office. And they also want to know what the President is like as a person: What are his tastes and preferences? Even, where does he go for a haircut? The kids want to feel as if they know him. They want him to be more than a military leader and a politician; they're looking for a special kind of person who is a connecting link for all Americans, someone who we all know in a genuine way. The youngsters want to feel that President Bush cares about each and every one of them, and that he is close to what we are all experiencing in our cities, towns, and neighborhoods.

For example, Dan T., age nine, commented during his interview: "President Bush should come to the schools more if he wants to stop drugs. He should show he is against dope but also show that he is interested in what problems kids have." Marvin, age ten, added: "A President shouldn't be like a king who just stays in the royal palace. He's got to go out there and mix with the people."

(2) YOUNG PEOPLE POKE FUN AT OUR LEADERS IN ORDER TO KEEP US FROM TAKING OURSELVES TOO SERIOUSLY. Whenever childhood humor is intentional, the humor can have a variety of purposes. Very often there is a serious message conveyed along with the entertaining content. With the children, I often felt that there was a subtle agenda behind the joke that was being made. In addition to "cutting up" with me or with their classmates, the youngsters also seem to be poking fun at the politics and government they see before them. They see a great deal of zaniness and irony in political life, and they seem to be saying: "Those politicians are pretty silly sometimes!"

Their explicit use of humor indicates that the children want the lighter and more human side of leadership fully recognized. In their anecdotes about insecure or manipulative Presidents, the children suggest that they have little use for unbridled self-importance. In response to my questions and in their spontaneous comments as well, many youngsters took it upon themselves to point out political hypocrisy. They took a certain pleasure in reducing larger-than-life figures to realistic size, especially if they sensed phoniness or self-interest. In one interview, ten-year-old Keith commented: "A President shouldn't tell the rest of the people he has to raise their taxes when he gets to use a lot of stuff at the White House without paying taxes for them. Like he uses the swimming pool, I'll bet. But he doesn't pay any taxes for it."

What some kids lack in tact, they certainly make up for in color! But the children are actually acting in accordance with the American tradition of poking fun at our leaders. Perhaps they, too, don't want any single figure to be greater or more important than America as a whole. Good-natured humor is a means that we adults have relied upon for two centuries to keep the Presidency in proper perspective, so in actuality, the youngsters are staying true to their American heritage.

(3) THE CHILDREN EXPRESS A NATURAL AND SINCERE EGALITARIANISM. Despite the diversity of the youngsters' responses, we find only a few comments that tend toward totalitarianism. Some youngsters aspire to be world rulers, dictators, or just plain monarchs (e.g., one youngster wanted to annex Canada and Mexico by force). These memorable exceptions are more than balanced by the many children who show empathy for their fellow men. In fact, most children show a decided interest in making the world a better and more egalitarian place. They look to the Presidency for help and direction in that regard. They want the President to make sure *everyone* is taken care of.

This wish comes through most clearly with respect to the subject that greed could easily dominate: money and economic matters. Many youngsters express a compelling interest in helping the poor and disadvantaged, especially children, and often invited the President to lead the way. Most cannot understand how things got to be so unequal, and they figure that the President must have the answer. Of course, a few youngsters are resourceful enough to offer some of their own creative suggestions. While these home remedies may not always be feasible (e.g., lowering all taxes to a penny a year), the youngsters' hearts are certainly in the right place. Their concern is genuine, and so is their frustration about not knowing how to help.

Homelessness has now become a common focal point for their feelings and concerns about the poor. As the first younger generation to grow up with homelessness as such an explicit problem, these youngsters (and the urban ones in particular) are keenly aware of the human anguish and the social dilemmas involved.

The thought of troubled, wandering people on our nation's streets makes the children very, very sad. J.P., a ten-year-old boy, describes his feelings: "I feel like it could be me if I didn't have a good family or if I was just born poor. It ain't their fault they're on the street, but you just feel like they're dying when you look at them." While some youngsters find it hard to express their feelings so well, others speak up and wonder what, if anything, the government can do. Most are confused about why there are people out there on the street, and sometimes they vent their confusion and frustration through criticism. "It's all a big national scandal," says Amy, age eleven.

Yet there is some guarded hopefulness, too. The youngsters' belief in America helps many adopt a "can-do" attitude in the end. Most children thought that the problem of homelessness would eventually be improved, though few thought it would go away altogether. They seemed to think that all the publicity about the homeless would help, and people would feel so bad about it that eventually genuine answers would be found. "I don't think those people will be cold and hungry forever," optimistically notes Marvin, age ten.

(4) THE CHILDREN PLACE THE EMPHASIS ON DOMESTIC CONCERNS IN GENERAL AND DRUGS IN PARTICULAR. Their concern about the homeless exemplifies just how important domestic issues are to the children. While concern about war and terrorism abroad are evident too, it's the problems that occur right around a child's own life that are the most gripping and frightening. Many of the children feel that this should be President Bush's foremost concern. "Drugs are our biggest problem," says thirteen-year-old Denny, " 'cause you'll never make it to college if you're all strung out. The President has got to do something about drugs if he wants to be the education President!" The attitudes of children like Denny are not insular or parochial but far more practical in nature: the children have observed many problems right around their neighborhoods, and they want them to change.

Yet what particularly disturbed this adult interviewer was that child after child seemed to view drugs and alcohol abuse as an entrenched part of society and modern life. They were convinced that drugs were here to stay. They saw no end to the problem in sight, and when questioned in fuller detail, could not really visualize an end. Born between 1976 and 1983, these young people had only known an America riddled with rampant drug use. Even in their lighthearted responses, one can detect an alarming familiarity with the drug culture. Crack was as much a part of their vocabulary as Cracker Jacks. The inner-city kids may have been the most conversant about the drug problem, but the suburban kids were far from naive. Drugs were on the minds of so many in a way that children shouldn't have to bear, and that distressing thought has stayed with me long after the interviews were completed.

(5) SOME AMERICAN STRENGTHS AND WEAKNESSES ARE EXPLORED. Whenever they talked about their pride in America, it was the element of freedom that children emphasized again and again. Unquestionably the children were exercising that freedom in the way they openly and even outrageously talked about the President. What a joy to listen to them revel in their inalienable right to freedom of speech about their government! Most children seemed to picture the President as a guardian of that freedom or as a figure who would not interfere with it. For those youngsters who saw the President in a negative light, freedom was perhaps even more important—as they chastised, criticized, or complained about that fellow in office. "I like Bush, but I thought Reagan was a jerk," commented Dexter, age thirteen, "but it's good we can say things like that and get away with it." "I like how everyone gets to vote. . . . Jeezus, even I'll get to vote soon!" adds twelve-year-old Priscilla H.

What seemed to irk the children the most was political selfishness and political self-absorption. They saw presidential campaigns as colorful but mostly incomprehensible, and they seemed to pick up on negative campaigning tactics, looking on them with disdain. Some kids found it hard to take the election process seriously (e.g., "It's all a big joke because they just want to win and don't care like they say they care"—Paul, age twelve). Others took a crack at party politics and used that as the butt of their jokes. Thirteen-year-old André observes: "I thought Bush and Dukakis acted like donkeys. They should be trying to act like Presidents. I hope next time the election is more mature."

(6) THE CHILDREN SPECULATE ON THE PRESIDENCY OF THE FUTURE. Based on their responses to the question "What will the President be like in the year 2000?" and other relevant questions, I found two common expectations that children had about the Presidency of the future.

When asked to reach into their crystal balls and have their turn at political clairvoyance, youngsters demonstrate a nice mixture of reason and imagination: They seem to feel that the future Presidents will have to be more technical and scientific, men or women at home and comfortable with modern systems and technologies. The youngsters didn't believe that the Presidents would necessarily be any younger, but they would be at the cutting edge of modern advances and societal changes. In a sense, the kids seemed to be depicting a "postcomputer-age" President, a person who is less of a career politician and more of a Renaissance person for the twenty-first century. "He'll have to be able to do lot of things," concludes nine-year-old Selina, "because all the paperwork around him will be multiplied times ten! He might even have to give orders to robot computers, so he'll have to know how to talk to them."

Yet these young people also foresee the need for an exceedingly moral person to be at the helm of America in the year 2000. Through their responses, they emphasize that the Presidents will have to be experienced moral decision-makers. The kids recognize that societal needs and viewpoints will be even more diverse and conflictual than they are now. "The President will have a lot of headaches if he's not careful," surmises eleven-year-old Julius. "He'll have to work till eleven o'clock at night!" contributes eight-year-old Paul.

When it comes to morality and values, the children were conservative about the type of person they were looking for. They may have wanted a space-conscious and scientific leader for the next century, but they sure don't want that to happen at the expense of basic American values. They saw the President's job as adhering to those values. They wanted a decent person with considerable wisdom and moral vision. Here are a few additional comments:

> In the year 2000, it could be a man or it could a woman. But either way, it will have to be someone who cares about all the people and who understands them all. (CHRISSIE, AGE 10)

> The President might have to make some real tough decisions about wars, so telling right from wrong will be a big deal. (LIZ, AGE 8)

People will be so many colors that the President then can't have no prejudice at all. (OSCAR, AGE 8)

The President will have to be a very nice person. That, I'm sure of! (C.J., AGE 6)

(7) THE DISCERNIBLE PRESENCE OF AN AMERICAN SPIRIT IS EVIDENT AMONG THE CHILDREN.   My final observation concerns a phenomenon that is difficult to put into words. It was something I felt in just being with the children and spending time with them, as much as what they explicitly said or wrote. It concerns the spirit that the children embody. There's a uniquely American spirit in their attitudes and manner, and it's so familiar that we as adults could easily take it for granted.

Unquestionably these kids have adopted some of our own adult skepticism and disillusionment about political life, and they can be very pragmatic about America, too. Yet they still retain a belief in a country that is tied to deeper ideals, a belief that transcends doubt about the President and our nation's leaders. And it's more sophisticated than a simplistic "My country, right or wrong." These children may not be able to list all the Presidents in order (how many of us can?) or have all their American history facts straight, but they do have a pretty good idea of what America means to them. They see America in terms of basic questions. Is it a good place to live? Does everyone have a fair chance? Do our leaders care about us? Can we make changes if we need to? They may come up with some mixed and inconclusive answers to these questions sometimes, but they press on and manage to be optimistic about America.

Where does their optimism come from? Perhaps it comes from a sense they have that our foundation is good and secure. Perhaps it's because they have faith in an enduring and well-meaning people. Timothy K., age twelve, comments: "The United States of America represents a lot to the world, 'cause it's a democracy and it's lasted a long time and it's kept the world okay against dictators." The children seem to rely upon their American roots and lean upon them as a source of strength and sustenance. They may joke about General Washington or Honest Abe, but deep down, these youngsters have internalized American folklore and taken it to heart. Undaunted by our modern ups and downs, and even our plaguing social problems, these young people carry with them an American spirit that is vibrant and resolute. "We'll be okay, just like whenever we have had tough times," assures ten-year-old Claire. "Even when we were just a bunch of patriots, we stayed together and made the democracy work."

Such spirit emerged frequently during the interviews, as well as throughout the children's comments, letters, and drawings. In their spirit we can see an America beyond Democrats and Republicans, and beyond all our ethnic and racial differences, to the society the colonists originally intended. It's a society based on time-honored ideals and capable of tolerating and encouraging many voices—most notably the wee voices of six- and seven- and eight-year-olds who are just learning about what a President does and what a Constitution is.

How quickly the children learn these things about our country! We can take great comfort and pride in that. The fundamental lessons of the American experience are being passed along, however quietly. But how these ideals will emerge in the next century—in what creative shapes and colors these young people will choose to paint their America—are questions that only they can answer.

Yet after spending a good deal of time with them and listening to their values and viewpoints, I am convinced that their America will be no less strong or sturdy—just a bit more philosophical and a whole lot more lighthearted. These children will be prepared for leadership, and they will make their own special mark on our national legacy.

As the project has come to its end, I have wondered if there's a future senator or a Cabinet member or even a future President among my young interviewees. I don't know for sure, but if there is such a person hidden among the stories and letters, then I know his or her Presidency or tenure will be an interesting one indeed! That youngster might change the color of the White House or reshape the bureaucracy, but if he or she does it with the same kind of purity that the kids have shown throughout, then we'll all be better off. Let's hope that the kids don't lose that purity as they grow up—and that America, in turn, doesn't either.

BOO!

Mr. President